JOURNEY TO IMPOSSIBLE PLACES

BOOK 1 · THE FALL

TED DEKKER & H.R. HUTZEL

ISBN (Paperback Edition): 979-8-9865173-3-9

Also Available in the Journey to Impossible Places trilogy:

The Great Divide (Book Two)
ISBN: 979-8-9865173-4-6 (Paperback Edition)

Redemption (Book Three)
ISBN: 979-8-9865173-5-3 (Paperback Edition)

Published by:

Scripturo
350 E. Royal Lane, Suite 150
Irving, TX 75039

Cover art and design by Manuel Preitano

Printed in the United States of America

CHAPTER ONE

CHARLIE LINGERED at the bathroom sink, watching the soap suds rinse from his fingers and disappear down the drain. He silently coached himself, as he did every morning, and contemplated how today might be better than yesterday—and the day before. Three months had passed since his arrival at Saint Francis's Boys and Girls Home, but Charlie's new life was not as perfect as he'd imagined.

The faucet knob gave a familiar squeak when he turned off the water. He quickly dried his hands, knowing he had mere minutes before he was due in his first class. But when he grabbed his books from the shelf beside the bathroom mirror, his golden-brown eyes caught his gaze in the reflection.

At thirteen years old, Charlie was the smallest of the kids his age at the orphanage. He was even shorter than some of the kids younger than him, like Milo. Charlie was hopeful he'd hit his growth spurt soon.

He straightened his tie, noting the way the bright-white collared shirt he wore as a part of his uniform contrasted with his brown skin. Foster siblings at one home had teased him for his skin tone. At least at this orphanage he wasn't the only person of color. Initially, he'd been self-conscious of his medium-brown skin. He wasn't dark like Kurtis or golden brown like Michael—just somewhere in between.

"But what's so bad about being different?" he asked his reflection.

All the kids at the home were unique in their own way. Still, Charlie couldn't help but compare himself to the others. Each one had their own set of talents. In comparison to them, Charlie felt pretty average.

Unremarkable was the word his last foster mother had used to described him to Mr. Abbott.

Mr. Abbott was the owner and founder of Saint Francis's Boys and Girls Home, a prestigious and exclusive orphanage located in the mountains of Montana. Charlie was thrilled when he'd received the invitation to join the sprawling ranch. He'd even enjoyed the envious expressions of Chloe and Ethan—two of the other foster children who lived with him.

For the first time in his life, Charlie had been chosen.

A flicker of light drew Charlie's eyes to the upper

left-hand corner of the mirror. Behind him, a glowing butterfly drifted through the boys' bathroom. Charlie turned to watch it float past the row of sinks and land on the sill of the window at the end of the bathroom.

He stared at it for a long time, blinking as he always did to see if it would disappear.

But it didn't.

Just like every other time, the glowing butterfly remained.

And Charlie was somehow the only person who could see it.

Behind him, the bathroom door burst open.

Charlie jumped. His books fell from his arms and landed with a loud thud.

Michael entered.

"Hey, Chucky," Michael said with a snicker. Charlie hated to be called that. "We've been looking for you." Michael looked at Charlie suspiciously, then glanced at the window. "Staring at imaginary glowing butter-flies again?"

Charlie mentally kicked himself for having told anyone at this orphanage about his weird butterfly sightings. He'd thought the kids here might be differ-ent, but of course that wasn't the case.

Michael's best friend, Tyler, entered the bathroom as well. The blond fourteen-year-old walked through the restroom and pushed open the doors to the four stalls. After confirming no one was there, he joined Michael beside Charlie at the mirror.

"Man, is it just me, or is Chucky getting shorter?" Tyler rested an elbow on top of Charlie's head and smashed his black curls against his scalp.

Looking at their reflections in the mirror, Michael looked Charlie up and down. He took a step closer, highlighting their height difference. "It's hard to say," Michael said. "You know, since we're still growing, and Charlie isn't." Michael narrowed his hazel-green eyes. "But I'd say he's definitely getting shorter." He slapped Charlie a little too hard on the shoulder.

"And uglier," Tyler added.

Michael shrugged, then ran a hand over his light-brown curls.

Charlie composed himself with a deep breath, knelt to collect his books, then tried to push past Michael.

"Where are you off to in such a hurry?" Michael asked. He stepped between Charlie and the door.

Michael was the same age as Charlie, but no one would ever guess it. Michael's face had already begun to transform into the more chiseled look of a young man, while Charlie's cheeks remained round and youthful.

Charlie straightened his shoulders and cleared his throat. "I'm headed to religion class. But you knew that."

Of course Michael knew. He had the same class schedule as Charlie—as did all the kids. There were only ten of them.

"I can't be late," Charlie added.

"Oh right, I almost forgot," Michael said with feigned ignorance. "You're still under observation for …" He tapped his chin. "How much longer do you have?"

Charlie hesitated then said, "Nine months."

"Nine months!" Michael whistled. "You still have nine whole months to maintain your perfect little attendance record?" Michael glanced at Tyler over the top of Charlie's head. "That's a long time, isn't it, Ty?"

"Sure is." Tyler chuckled.

"And you don't have a single mark against you?" Michael asked. "Attendance or behavior?"

Charlie lowered his eyes. Heat rose within him, but he stuffed his anger. He wouldn't allow Michael to get under his skin. Through gritted teeth, Charlie said, "Michael, can you please just let me get to class?"

Michael tipped Charlie's chin up, but Charlie refused to look at him. "You don't have to be so rude, Chucky," Michael said. "We're just trying to have a polite conversation with you. That's what family does, you know."

Charlie allowed his gaze to meet Michael's.

"But, of course, you're not family—*yet*." Michael sneered.

Charlie winced. Michael was right. Though Charlie had been allowed into Saint Francis's Boys and Girls Home, he did not yet belong.

During his brief orientation, Charlie had the pleasure of meeting Mr. Abbott in person. The man explained that, typically, children came to the orphanage when they were six years old or younger. Charlie was the first exception to this rule.

When Charlie had asked Mr. Abbot why he'd made the exception, the kind man said: "I look for certain qualities when selecting the children I want to be a part of my family. I have my hunches about you, Charlie." The man smiled broadly. "We'll see if I'm right. To date, I haven't been wrong about this kind of thing."

Mr. Abbott went on to explain that each child underwent a rigorous onboarding process, which included a one-year probationary period to prove their worth. After that year, he would legally adopt the children who had conformed to his high standards, and they would have the privilege of growing up as members of the Abbott family.

The thought thrilled Charlie. Having never known his father or mother, all he'd ever wanted was to be part of a family. After thirteen years of foster care, Charlie believed Mr. Abbott's offer was a dream come true. As he'd walked the grounds with Mr. Abbott on his first day at the ranch, Charlie realized that Saint Francis's Boys and Girls Home was beyond his wildest dreams.

The picturesque modern ranch was situated on a vast plain surrounded by mountainous views. The main house was a mansion by Charlie's standards, with a small, private bedroom for each of the ten children who lived there. Charlie had never had his own bedroom before. A modern classroom, massive kitchen, well-stocked library, and shared boys' and girls' bathrooms completed the main house. But for Charlie, the highlight of the orphanage was the land.

During Charlie's first day on the premises, Mr. Abbott had walked him from the main house to the barn, where five horses were stabled for the children's weekly riding lessons. An in-ground pool, tennis court, and archery range lay beyond the pasture, where two children were shooting arrows at the targets. One of them was Michael.

Charlie wasn't sure why, but from the moment Michael laid eyes on him, he'd marked Charlie as his enemy.

Fortunately, Charlie had become quick friends with Sarah. She'd told Charlie that Michael was hard on all the newcomers. But despite Sarah's attempts to put his mind at ease, Charlie knew Michael had reserved a special kind of hatred just for him.

The bullying became so bad that Charlie began to wonder if fighting for his place in the Abbott family was worth it. He'd dealt with bullies before, but never anyone as sinister as Michael.

If it had been any other orphanage or foster situation, Charlie would have tried to transfer. But whenever he recalled his meeting with Mr. Abbott, Charlie knew this was the place he longed to call home—even if it meant he had to put up with Michael.

Charlie hadn't seen Mr. Abbott since his first day of orientation. Sarah explained that this was typical. Mr. Abbott wasn't around much and often away on business. The nuns at Saint Francis's Boys and Girls Home handled the day-to-day care of the children and their education.

"One-on-one time with Mr. Abbott is a rarity," Sarah had said. "You should feel lucky he spent so much time with you during your orientation. He must really like you."

Charlie did count himself lucky in that regard.

Charlie smoothed his hand over his curly hair and mustered some confidence. "I need to get to class," he said to Michael. "Excuse me."

Michael thrust his hands into his pockets and shrugged. Charlie could tell that there was something in the left one. "All right. Get out of here then."

Charlie shifted to the right to go around him, but Michael blocked his path. Charlie moved left.

"Go on," Michael harassed. "You don't want to be late."

Charlie clenched his jaw, started for the right again, then quickly darted left only to slam into Michael's now upheld hand, which gripped a red permanent marker. The cap was off.

"Oh no," Michael said.

Charlie could hear the amusement in his voice.

"You've got something on your shirt, Chucky." Michael tapped the open tip of the marker to the breast pocket of Charlie's white button-down shirt. "It's right *there*." He tapped again for emphasis.

Charlie glanced down to see the bloodred color seep into the fabric of his shirt. The mark was directly above the embroidered crest of the orphanage. Charlie's stomach dropped.

Michael pressed the marker's tip to the fabric again and allowed the ink to soak the pocket. Charlie could do nothing but stare. Behind him he heard Tyler chuckle.

"Oh no, Chucky." Michael tsked. "I'm afraid your perfect record has a mark." A grin spread over Michael's face. "And not just any mark, a big fat *F*."

Michael dragged the marker over the white space

above the crest and drew a bright-red letter *F* on the front of Charlie's shirt.

"*F* is for *family*," Michael said in a sing-song voice.

He drew over his original lines, making the *F* even bolder.

"Which you'll never be."

He smiled and darkened the lines a third time.

"And *F* is for *failure*." Michael bored his eyes into Charlie's. "You know, like you."

He didn't even peel his gaze from Charlie's as he pulled the marker over his shirt one final time.

"And *F* is for *forgotten*. Because that's what's going to happen to you once I get you kicked out of this place. Everyone will forget you. Especially me."

Michael capped the marker and tucked it into Charlie's breast pocket.

Tyler's laughter echoed off the tiled bathroom walls.

Charlie turned his eyes down to his ruined shirt.

Michael slapped him on the shoulder and turned for the door. "See you later, Chucky. Tyler and I need to get to class."

As soon as they were out of the bathroom, Charlie ripped off his tie and pulled his shirt over his head. He pumped the hand soap at least a dozen times and saturated the fabric. Frantically, he scrubbed the material with his fingernails, but the ink from the marker only bled. The letter *F* was still visible.

"C'mon," he muttered. "C'mon."

Sarah's voice replayed in his mind. She was the one who'd told Charlie how important it was to keep his uniform in pristine condition. Mr. Abbott valued first impressions.

Charlie turned on the hot water and shoved the shirt under the stream, careful not to soak the entire garment. Red water hit the basin and swirled down the drain, but the letter *F* was still clearly there. He tried cold water next. But that made it seem worse. After thirty more seconds scrubbing with soap and water, Charlie had a partially wet shirt with a pink ring and a slightly less red *F*.

The bell rang as he began to dry the shirt under the hand dryer.

Charlie squeezed his eyes shut. He was officially late for class.

Sighing, he yanked several paper towels out of the dispenser and blotted the shirt as best he could. He yanked it over his head, grabbed his books and tie, and darted into the hall.

Outside the classroom door, Charlie adjusted his books against his chest and tried to cover the giant stain. It was no use. Sister Cecile would see it at some point. Besides, he hadn't had time to tuck in his shirt or put on his tie, which he'd draped over his arm.

He drew a deep breath and entered the room. Sister Cecile clocked him immediately.

"Charlie, nice of you to join us." She flashed him an odd look but clearly hadn't seen the stain yet. "You're late. And looking a bit disheveled, I might add." Her voice was stern. "I'm afraid this will have to be the first mark on your record." She eyed him up and down. "Perhaps two. Please take your seat."

Charlie walked swiftly to his desk in the second row and plopped down into the seat. He could feel the eyes of the nine other students on him. Especially Michael's.

He set his books on his desk, folded his arms across his chest, and tried to angle his shoulders forward. But he couldn't hide the stain. Sister Cecile faced the interactive whiteboard at the front of the room.

"Class, please open your Bibles to Luke chapter six. We'll begin with verse twenty-seven." The passage flashed onto the screen. "Who would like to read today's scripture passage aloud?" Sister Cecile turned as she spoke. Her eyes landed on Charlie. "Oh my."

Charlie stared at his desk as she approached.

"Charlie, what happened to your shirt?" Concern tinged her question.

From the corner of his eye, Charlie could see Michael staring at him. The anger he felt toward Michael flared in his gut.

"Charlie?" Sister Cecile repeated. "Please answer me. What happened to your shirt?" She leaned down for a closer inspection. "Who did this to you?"

Charlie swallowed his rage. "No one," he said under his breath.

"No one?" There was a hint of surprise in Sister Cecile's voice. "So you did this to yourself then? You drew on your own shirt?"

Charlie worked his jaw back and forth and noticed Sarah turn in her seat in front of him. She gave him a sympathetic glance.

Silently she mouthed, *Michael?*

Of course it had been Michael. Even Sister Cecile probably suspected it was him. But years in foster care had taught Charlie that it was usually best not to rat out a bully. Doing so often only ensured things would be much worse for him the next time.

And there was always a next time.

Charlie bit his tongue.

"Charlie." Sister Cecile crouched beside his desk and lowered her voice. "Clearly you didn't do this to your own shirt. I want to help you, but you have to tell me what happened." She paused and allowed the silence to linger. Charlie returned his stare to the top of his desk. Another several agonizing seconds passed before she finally said, "Fine. If you won't stand up for yourself, then responsibility for this failure will fall on you."

F is for failure. Michael's words echoed in Charlie's mind.

"That's three marks, Charlie." Sister Cecile stood and returned to the front of the classroom. He saw her write something in the notebook on her desk. "As I'm sure you recall, you're only allowed ten. You'd better pace yourself. You have nine months before your final evaluation." She closed the notebook. "In addition, you'll spend your recreation time this afternoon with Sister Margarette, learning how to remove marker from your clothing." Her expression was more pitying than empathetic. She stared at him a long moment before she turned back to the Bible verse on the whiteboard. "I suppose this is a fitting passage for today." Her eyes scanned the classroom. "Maxine, why don't you read for us?"

On the right side of the classroom, a nine-year-old girl with soft brown hair stood beside her desk. She picked up her Bible, flipped to the passage and began to read in a sweet voice. "But to you who are listening I say: Love your enemies, do good to those who hate you, bless those who curse you, pray for those who mistreat you. If someone slaps you on one cheek, turn to them the other also. If someone takes your coat, do not withhold your shirt from them. Give to everyone who asks you, and if anyone takes what belongs to you, do not demand it back. Do to others as you would have them do to you."

Without meaning to, Charlie glanced at Michael. The bully's face was expressionless, but there was hatred in his eyes.

"If you love those who love you, what credit is that to you?" Maxine's voice filled the classroom. "Even sinners love those who love them. And if you do good to those who are good to you, what credit is that to you? Even sinners do that."

Charlie turned to stare straight ahead. Maxine's voice faded from his awareness.

Love his enemies? Even Michael? Charlie had tried that, but his kindness was met with death-stares and mean comments. When that didn't work, he'd tried to ignore Michael, which only made things worse. No matter what Charlie did, Michael hated him. And Charlie had no idea why.

Maxine continued. "Love your enemies, do good to them, and lend to them without expecting to get anything back. Then your reward will be great, and you will be children of the Most High, because he is kind to the ungrateful and wicked. Be merciful, just as your Father is merciful." She paused. "Should I stop there?"

"Why don't you continue through verse forty-two?" Sister Cecile said.

Maxine nodded. "Do not judge, and you will not

be judged. Do not condemn, and you will not be condemned. Forgive, and you will be forgiven—"

"Excuse me?" A man's voice interrupted Maxine.

Everyone looked up to see Father Martin in the classroom doorway, a rare sight for sure. Young, single, and fit, Father Martin was responsible for managing the estate in addition to the chapel. The children rarely saw him near the classroom.

"I'm so sorry to interrupt your morning studies," Father Martin said, "but I have some exciting news. May I come in?"

"Of course," Sister Cecile said. She waved him into the classroom.

"I just got off a call with Mr. Abbott," Father Martin began. "He informed me that an anonymous benefactor reached out to him to say how much he loves our mission here at Saint Francis's Boys and Girls Home."

Intrigued, Charlie leaned forward in his seat.

"This particular benefactor works with several orphanages in Mexico, one of them in Cozumel. He wants to send all ten of the children down for a three-day community service trip to take supplies to the kids in Mexico and help them with some projects. And …" Father Martin paused dramatically. A smile pulled at his lips as he turned his attention to the children. "And then let you stay there an additional three days for a vacation! You leave in two days."

The classroom came alive with enthusiastic chatter and cheers.

Sarah, eyes wide, turned around to face Charlie. "Can you believe it? A vacation!"

Charlie forced a smile onto his face and nodded. Sarah quickly turned in her seat to face Becca. The two of them chattered away.

A vacation. Charlie had never been on a vacation before. None of his previous foster families had ever included him in their family trips.

Charlie glanced over at Michael, who was busy talking with Tyler. It seemed Charlie's situation might finally be turning in the right direction. He knew he wasn't a part of the family yet, but for the first time in his life, Charlie was going on a family vacation.

CHAPTER TWO

THE SCENT OF OLD BOOKS filled Charlie's nostrils as he drew a deep breath. Anticipation for the upcoming adventure flooded his body—along with a hint of anxiety. He stared out the window of the library at the private jet parked in the open field in front of the house. Its white exterior gleamed against the mountain backdrop as it waited to take all ten children, along with Sister Cecile, on their impromptu trip.

Charlie perched in the window seat and watched the pilot load their luggage onto the plane. He watched nervously for his backpack but didn't see it.

"There you are." Sarah's familiar voice filled the library. "I've been looking for you." The sound of her footsteps approached from behind him. "Charlie? Are you okay?"

He turned to look at her. Dressed in her blue-and-green plaid skort and a white polo shirt, she looked ready for class, not a tropical vacation. Even her navy-blue uniform blazer was slung over one of her arms. She tucked her short black hair behind her ears and approached the window seat.

"Why are you in your uniform?" Charlie asked. "Sister Cecile said we don't have to wear them today since we're just traveling."

"I know." Sarah sat across from him in the seat and leaned back against the window casing. She followed his eyes to the plane. "It's habit, I guess. I like to make a good first impression. I think it's what Mr. Abbott would do, even if he were just traveling."

Charlie peered down at his plain white T-shirt and khaki shorts.

He glanced up and watched Sarah, her dark, thin eyes still fixed on the plane. "You never answered me," she said.

"Huh?"

She turned to look at him. "I asked if you were okay."

"Oh." Charlie faced the window again. "I don't know. I guess I'm pretty nervous."

"About the plane ride?" Sarah pulled her legs up onto the window seat and tucked them beneath her.

Finally, Charlie saw the pilot load his bag onto the jet. "Yeah. I've never flown before."

"Don't be nervous." Sarah reached out and touched his shoulder. "You'll love it."

"You've flown before?"

She nodded. "A few times, the longest when I transferred here. It was two long flights, actually. All the way from Japan."

Charlie nodded and remembered the brief memories Sarah had shared with him from her time at the orphanage in Japan. She was only five years old when Mr. Abbott brought her to the ranch. She'd told Charlie she didn't remember much else from her time before Saint Francis's Boys and Girls Home.

Charlie wished he had fewer memories of his time before transferring. Though he wasn't making better memories here—*yet*. Charlie continued to believe the Montana ranch could become his permanent residence. And that somehow, he'd convince Michael to accept him.

Or, at the very least, ignore him.

"Those planes were much bigger," Sarah continued. "Commercial flights. I've never been on a private jet before." Excitement lit up her face. "Sister Cecile said there's probably snacks and drinks on the plane—and a movie!"

Charlie nodded. "That would be cool …"

"But?"

Charlie sighed. "Heights make me nervous."

"Me too," Sarah said. "But it's different when you're on a plane. You'll see. Plus, we can sit together!"

Excitement lit her face, and Charlie couldn't help but feel his fear begin to fade.

"Oh, and one other thing." Sarah winced as if she was about to deliver bad news. "I caught Michael trying to empty an entire bottle of shampoo into your backpack."

Charlie felt his eyes go wide.

"Don't worry, I stopped him."

Charlie shook his head. "I don't get it. Why does he hate me so much?"

"That's just Michael," Sarah said. "He's like that with—"

"No." Charlie shifted to face Sarah fully. "He's not like that with everyone else. He's only like *that* with me. And you know it."

Sarah pressed her lips together and held his stare. "I know," she finally said.

Charlie nodded, happy she'd finally admitted what they both knew to be true. "So what is it then? Did I say something to him? Did I do something to make him hate me? Or is it just my overall existence he can't stand?" Irritation tinged Charlie's words. "Admit it, Sarah. Michael hates me." He lowered his voice. "And it's getting pretty hard to not hate him back."

"Don't say that," Sarah said. "You're better than that. In fact, it's probably one of the reasons Michael picks on you so much. You don't ever let him get under your skin."

"But he does."

"Well, you hide it well. It seems like no matter how hard he pushes, you refuse to react. You could have ratted him out to Sister Cecile the other day, but you didn't."

"That would have only made things worse."

"Maybe." Sarah shrugged. "Honestly, I think he's jealous of you."

A loud laugh escaped Charlie's lips. "Jealous? Of me?"

Sarah nodded, but Charlie couldn't stop laughing.

"It's not a joke," she said.

Charlie composed himself. "Sarah, there is no way Michael is jealous of me. Look at me." He gestured to his body. "There's nothing special about me." He raised his eyebrows. "In fact, I still can't figure out why Mr. Abbot wanted me here in the first place. I don't exactly fit in with the rest of you."

"Well, you do see glowing butterflies," Sarah said with a grin.

Charlie narrowed his eyes at her.

"I'm only kidding," she said. "I actually think it'd be pretty cool to see things other people can't. But back to Michael—this is exactly why he's jealous of you."

Charlie gave her a hard stare. "Because I see imaginary glowing butterflies?"

"No!" She laughed. "Because you're different, Charlie—in your own way. The rest of us were all brought here before the age of six. But you?" Sarah grinned. "You're the exception. And that threatens Michael."

"That seems like a stretch."

"It's not. Didn't you know that Michael was the first kid to come to the ranch? And the first Mr. Abbott adopted? Michael sees himself as the king of the castle." She shrugged. "And unfortunately, the rest of us have let him go on believing that. But you're a threat to his power." She used air quotes around the word *power*. "Don't you get it? You *are* special, Charlie. What makes you so special is the fact that you don't need to be special."

Charlie smirked. "I'm sure you mean that as a compliment, but it doesn't feel like one."

"That's okay." Sarah grinned. "You can thank me later." She jumped off the window seat, and her tennis shoes slapped against the worn wooden floorboards. She started for the door.

Charlie cast another glance out the window at the plane. "I just hope Michael doesn't make my life too miserable during our trip."

Sarah stopped in the doorway and turned. "Don't worry," she said. "I've got your back, Charlie. I know we're not family yet, but that's what friends do." She motioned for him to follow. "C'mon. We've got a plane to catch."

Charlie relaxed into the plush leather chair of the private jet, thankful he was finally able to enjoy the flight. It had taken a solid hour for him to release his death grip on the armrests, another hour before he'd dared to lift the window shade, and at least another hour before Sarah could convince him to watch a movie with her.

"Worrying doesn't help hold the plane in the air," she'd said.

She was right. Still, Charlie preferred to have the window shade down. He closed it during the movie.

Now, several hours and one refueling stop later, Charlie took a swig of his water, then turned to look at Sarah. She sat across the aisle from him, seat leaned back as far as it would go. Her knees bounced in rhythm with music he couldn't hear. She adjusted her earbuds, then caught his stare. She pulled one out of her ear.

"What?" she asked.

"You were right," Charlie said. "About flying."

She grinned. "I know."

Charlie placed the nearly empty water bottle in the cup holder beside a granola bar wrapper.

"About forty-five minutes till we land," Sarah said, glancing down at the time on her iPhone. "I can't wait to sink my toes into the sand on the beach."

"I've never been to the beach," Charlie said.

"Mr. Abbott took us to Florida a couple years ago," Sarah said. She raised her seat. "It was so much fun. Oh!" she said excitedly. "Maybe we can go bodyboarding in Cozumel. Or snorkeling! Mr. Abbott took us on several excursions in Florida. I wonder if Sister Cecile will set anything up for us."

Charlie glanced up the aisle to the front of the plane, where Sister Cecile sat in the first row. The seat beside her was filled with extra supplies they were transporting to the orphanage in Cozumel—a stack of tarps and blankets from what Charlie could see.

"I wish Mr. Abbott could have joined us," Charlie said.

Michael, who sat in the seat in front of Sarah, turned. "Mr. Abbott only joins us on *family* vacations," he said. He eyed Charlie up and down. "Clearly this isn't a family trip." He turned back around in his chair.

Charlie gritted his teeth.

"Ignore him," Sarah said.

Charlie sighed. "That's getting harder to do."

It was the first time Michael had spoken to Charlie since takeoff. In fact, the only other time Michael seemed to notice Charlie was when he caught him staring at the unusual star-shaped birthmark on Michael's right forearm. He'd shot Charlie a death stare, then rolled down the long sleeves of his green Hawaiian print shirt. Seated across the aisle from Michael, Tyler wore a similar shirt. His was blue. Charlie guessed they'd bought the matching shirts on their last beach vacation.

Sarah returned her earbuds to her ears, and Charlie leaned his head back against the headrest. He closed his eyes, imagining every beach picture he'd ever seen. He couldn't believe he was less than an hour away from wiggling his toes in the sand.

The white noise of the plane lulled Charlie into a trancelike state. He hadn't slept well the previous night, feeling nervous about the plane ride. But now, gliding smoothly through the air, he felt drowsy. Within seconds, his breathing slowed, and his chin dropped to his chest.

A jolt from the plane jarred Charlie upright, eyes wide.

The plane rumbled beneath him for a couple of agonizing seconds.

Sarah reached a hand across the aisle and touched

Charlie's forearm. She removed her earbuds with her other hand.

"It's just a bit of turbulence," she said. "It's perfectly normal."

Charlie nodded and slowly exhaled.

"We'll be there soon." Sarah flashed an exaggerated grin. She tapped the Play button on her iPhone and placed her earbuds in her ears.

The plane resumed its smooth course, and Charlie relaxed once again. He hesitated a moment, then reached over to push up the window shade. It took a moment for his eyes to adjust to the bright light, then his breath caught in his throat. A vast swath of deep turquoise-blue stretched as far as he could see in any direction. A surprising calm washed over Charlie. He'd glimpsed the ocean through Sarah's open window across the aisle, but it was another experience to peer down from his own. The view was stunning. He cast a glance over his shoulder to look at Sarah. She caught his eye and gave him an I-told-you-so grin. Charlie returned the smile, then turned back to the window.

A glowing butterfly floated outside.

Charlie blinked several times, then rubbed his eyes. The butterfly was still there.

Now Charlie *knew* he was crazy, just as Michael and everyone else had teased. It was impossible for a butterfly—of any kind—to fly at this altitude.

Wasn't it?

Charlie focused on the subtle flicker of its wings. It was a beautiful hallucination but a hallucination all the same. He'd been seeing them since he was a small boy—as far back as he could remember. The butterflies seemed to appear at random; one second, they'd be there; the next, they were gone.

Charlie fixed his eyes on the butterfly, resolved to see the exact moment it vanished.

Instead, the butterfly simply drifted away, fading from his vision like a real, physical insect.

Charlie scratched his head, cast another glance at Sarah to see if she'd noticed anything unusual, then turned back to his window.

When he did, the horizon line tilted.

The left side of the plane plunged but quickly righted itself. Charlie's stomach flipped. He heard someone scream.

The plane jolted, then dropped again, but a violent shake soon replaced the falling sensation.

Charlie's heart was in his throat. Sister Cecile turned in her seat and attempted to shout over the roar that filled the jet.

The pilot came over the loudspeaker. "Please remain calm," he said. His voice was hurried, tense, even jumbled. "As you can see, we're experiencing a bit of turbulence. Please fasten your seatbelts and return your seats to an upright position."

Charlie tightened his safety belt, then gripped the armrests.

The plane lurched again.

Oxygen masks dropped from the ceiling, and the pilot's voice returned.

"We're experiencing a change in cabin pressure." His voice was getting harder to hear. "Please secure your masks and breathe normally." The speaker crackled with static. The pilot's voice cut in and out. "Please secure your own mask before helping—"

Charlie couldn't hear what he said next. He tightened the strap of the oxygen mask around the back of his head. His breath came short and rapid. His heart thrummed against his chest.

Across the aisle, Sarah's face was white behind the yellow mask. She looked at Charlie, terrified.

More screams filled the cabin as the jet lolled from side to side.

Sister Cecile clutched her rosary.

The cabin lights flickered off and on, then off completely.

The plane dropped again. But this time, it kept dropping.

Charlie had only ridden one roller coaster in his

life. And he'd hated it. He couldn't stand the sensation of falling.

At least the roller coaster had a bottom. It seemed this plane ride did not.

Charlie dug his fingernails into the armrests.

The pilot came over the loudspeaker a final time. His words were clipped. "Please prepare for a water landing."

Charlie remembered the pilot had told them during the flight's takeoff about the life preservers under their seats. He never imagined he'd have to use one.

He tried to reach down and grasp the life vest, but his stomach was in his throat, his body forcibly pressed back into the seat. He couldn't move, only watch out his open window, where the once-serene sea now rushed toward him at a horrifying speed. He could make out the white caps on its surface.

The front of the plane sloped to an impossible angle. Bile crept up the back of Charlie's throat, his stomach now inside out. The sensation of falling overwhelmed him.

For a moment Charlie noticed how clear and unusual his thoughts were. Time seemed to slow. His brain latched on to unimportant details: the putrid yellow color of the oxygen masks; the way the leather seat stuck to the back of his sweaty legs.

A strange thought flitted across his mind: he wished

he'd worn his uniform, as Sarah had. That way he could make a good impression when they recovered his body.

If they recovered his body.

At thirteen years of age, Charlie had never considered what his final thoughts might be before his death. But these certainly wouldn't have been among his guesses. They didn't last long. The gravitational force of the plummeting plane soon became the only thing he could focus on. Violent shocks reverberated through the jet.

From the corner of his eye, Charlie took one last look at his best, and perhaps only, friend. Sarah's face was barely visible behind the oxygen mask, but Charlie could tell that she no longer enjoyed flying.

A flash of bright turquoise raced past the window on Charlie's left.

It was too close.

In one second, the most striking shade of blue Charlie had ever seen filled his view.

And in the next, it was black.

CHAPTER THREE

CHARLIE GASPED. His body lurched forward in his seat. He couldn't move. Chaos surrounded him. Screams filled his ears. Someone shouted his name, but all he could focus on was his immobile body. It was as if he were glued to the leather seat.

The plane sloped at a forty-five-degree angle, but it was no longer falling. Charlie's entire body thrummed from the force of the impact. It seemed to have knocked him unconscious for a time. Or perhaps the shock of the crash prevented Charlie from thinking straight. He watched the water level rise in the front of the plane. Already, the cockpit and first two rows of seats in the cabin were submerged. Water would reach him in mere seconds.

Hearing someone shout his name again, Charlie's brain finally made sense of why he couldn't move—his seatbelt. His fingers fumbled with the buckle. On the second try, he got it loose and stood. He had to hold on to the seat in front of him to keep from falling. It was already empty.

Charlie turned and saw Sarah still in her seat, slumped forward. Blood ran down her forehead and over her closed eyelids.

"Sarah!" She didn't move.

Water soaked his tennis shoes.

Charlie lunged across the aisle, ripped the seatbelt off her lap, and shook her shoulders. "Sarah! Wake up!"

Her eyes fluttered.

"Sarah!"

"Charlie!" Again, someone yelled his name. Charlie looked up and turned in the direction of the voice. Kurtis stood at the back of the plane, leaning against the open exit door. "This way!" he shouted, then dove out the back of the jet.

"Sarah! C'mon!" Charlie yanked her out of her chair. Sarah's iPhone slipped from her hand and dropped through the water that now encircled their waists. The drag of the quickly sinking plane tugged at their bodies.

Sarah was conscious but barely. Her arms flailed, but somehow Charlie managed to push her through the water and toward the exit. They had seconds before its opening would be submerged.

Only a foot of clearance remained when Charlie helped push Sarah out the open door. By the time he got her through, it was gone.

Charlie sucked in a huge gulp of air, then ducked beneath the surface. His fingers wrapped around the doorframe, legs kicking as he shoved off the plane and into open water. Seconds later, his head broke the surface.

Light pierced his eyes. He blinked against the salty burn.

Sarah floated on her back just outside the plane. She didn't move.

Thrusting his arms in front of him, Charlie swam toward her, looped his arm through one of hers, then kicked. In what direction it didn't matter, so long as it was away from the plane. If they were too close when it sank, it would drag them both into the grave.

The sounds of crashing waves and screaming children pierced his ears. The only words he could make out were, "Land! There's land! Swim!"

Charlie struggled to keep himself and Sarah afloat. He turned, searching in every direction until he saw it.

A beach rose from the gulf no more than fifty yards away. He pulled Sarah's body in that direction, trying to keep her mouth and nose out of the water. Wet hair plastered her pale face.

Charlie's legs burned. His lungs sucked air. Panic gripped him as he wondered if he could make it.

He scanned the scene for the rest of his classmates

and Sister Cecile, but the waves buffeted him and fought to drag him beneath the surface. Saltwater sprayed into his eyes.

The shore was closer now. Already Charlie could see several kids hauling their bodies onto the beach.

Not daring to glance back at the plane, he forced his one free arm in front of him and clung to Sarah with the other. His mind fixed on one thought: he had to get Sarah to shore.

Another wave battered him from behind. Charlie's head dipped. The next surge pulled him under and ripped Sarah from his grip.

Beneath the swell, Charlie tumbled. A sharp burning sensation gushed up his nose. The saltwater filled his sinus cavity and rushed down the back of his throat. Disoriented, he tried to surface, but another wave pummeled him again. The sea tossed him like a ragdoll and knocked him against its sandy bottom. The abrasive surface scraped his arms and legs.

His body collided with Sarah's when the ocean hurled him again.

Lungs burning, Charlie locked his fingers around her wrist. He finally managed to get his feet under him and shoved up from the ocean floor toward the surface. The water wasn't deep here, but the waves beat harder now. And Sarah had been unconscious for too long.

Finally, Charlie reached a place where his feet could touch. He dug his tennis shoes into the sandy bottom and pulled Sarah's body to shore. Dropping to his knees, he began chest compressions while she was still partially in the water.

Sarah coughed violently. Water spewed from her mouth. She gasped.

Charlie pulled her all the way up onto the sand, then collapsed beside her, silently thanking a previous foster mother for requiring all the children in her care to learn CPR.

Charlie rolled onto his back and stared at the bright-blue sky. His chest heaved. He waited for his breathing to slow, then shoved up to a seated position.

Sarah lay beside him, clutching her chest. Her eyes were wide with horror. She reached over and grasped Charlie's arm.

Adrenaline coursed through his veins. He scanned the beach, seeing several other children clutching the sandy earth as he and Sarah now did. He turned. A tropical rainforest lined the beach not thirty yards behind them.

"Tyler! Please just swim out there!"

Charlie snapped his head in the direction of the voice.

Becca stood at the water's edge, shouting at Tyler,

who stood frozen in the ankle-deep brownish-green waves, staring at the plane. It was as if he couldn't hear her.

"Tyler!" she shouted again. "Sister Cecile isn't on the beach. And neither is the pilot. Someone has to go back for them. You're the strongest swimmer."

Finally Tyler glanced over his shoulder at Becca. His eyes were unfocused, but he nodded. He stripped off his shirt and shoes, then waded out into the deep. The tail end of the plane jutted from the water.

Charlie tried to jump to his feet, but he nearly toppled when he took his first step. His legs felt like rubber.

Sarah caught his arm. "Where are you going?"

"I need to help Tyler." Charlie tried to yank his arm away. His body felt so weak.

Sarah's eyes widened. "Don't leave me!"

Charlie cast another glance at Tyler then nodded. His entire body thrummed with fatigue. He would be no help anyway.

Sarah extended her other hand, and Charlie helped her to her feet.

Together, they scanned the beach. All the kids had made it out of the plane.

They were alive.

Sarah pointed. "There's Maxine."

The young girl stood in the surf, arms wrapped around her waist, sobbing. Sarah rushed to console her.

Charlie joined the rest of the group and took a seat beside Kurtis, who sat frozen in the sand, his watch clutched between his fingers.

No one spoke. Not even Michael, who was slightly apart from them, knees drawn to his chest, eyes fixed on the plane. His golden-brown skin—normally a shade or two lighter than Charlie's—looked pale and ashen. Even his hair looked drained of color, the sun bringing out the blond ends of his curls. He turned his head toward Charlie. Sunlight reflected off the water and highlighted the features of Michael's face. Charlie had never seen him look so scared.

Michael turned back to the water where Tyler approached.

Hands on his hips, Tyler stared at the waves that crashed around his ankles. A drenched backpack hung from his shoulder. He stood beside Michael, but neither of them spoke.

For several long minutes, the only sounds they heard were the crash of the violent surf and Maxine's muffled sobs.

Eventually, Becca said, "Is everyone okay? Is anyone hurt?"

For the first time since he pulled himself out of the

water, Charlie glanced down at his body. His arms were skinned from being tossed against the bottom of the ocean. Bruises had already begun to form on his knees.

Still in shock, he hadn't noticed the thin trickle of blood that seeped from the small gash above Sarah's eyebrow. Her bottom lip was swollen and split.

"I hit my head on something during the crash," Sarah said. "But I think I'm okay, thanks to Charlie." She glanced over at him, her smile forced. Fear lingered in her eyes.

Charlie nodded. His head hurt. Maybe he'd hit something too—he couldn't remember. He'd been too focused on helping Sarah get to land to take note of his own injuries. But now, the memory of the swim to shore blipped in and out like a senseless dream. In fact, the whole horrifying event felt fuzzy and surreal. Had they really crashed?

Charlie took note of the rest of their group. Each child had a unique set of scrapes and bruises, but no one was in imminent danger. Not even Raegan, who cupped a large gash on her forearm. Bright-red blood pooled around her palm and dripped down her fair skin.

Charlie noticed that Michael hadn't moved from his spot, his eyes still glued to the tail of the plane.

Tyler swung the dripping-wet backpack from his

shoulders and dropped it into the sand.

Becca stared at him for a long moment, as if she wasn't sure she wanted to ask the question they were all wondering. "Well?" she said. "Sister Cecile? The pilot?"

"Are they dead?" Maxine asked. Her voice quivered.

Charlie felt his stomach drop.

Tyler shook his head, eyes fixed on the sand at his feet. "I don't know. They weren't on the plane. I guess I didn't get out there fast enough."

Charlie could tell from Tyler's expression that his thoughts were swirling. As with Michael, it was the first time Charlie had seen Tyler scared or lost. The older boy blinked a couple times, then composed himself. He shot Charlie a glare when he noticed him staring.

"It's okay, Tyler," Maxine said. She touched his arm. "You helped me get to the beach."

Tyler's face remained emotionless, but he ruffled the top of Maxine's head and said, "That's right, Squirt. I wouldn't have left you behind."

"So, where are they then?" Sarah asked.

"They have to be somewhere!" Raegan shouted, her words tinted with anxiety. Her strawberry-blonde hair hung in long wet tendrils down her back. She was thirteen, but standing in a soaked T-shirt and dripping shorts, she looked much younger. They all did.

Charlie could read the fear on each face. They were

in shock. His mind whirled with confusion, but he fought to be an anchor for the group.

"Look," Charlie began, "I know we're all confused and scared, but we can't panic. That's the worst thing we can do right now."

Michael's head snapped in Charlie's direction. "Don't tell us what to do." His voice was hard and cold.

Charlie couldn't form a reply.

Raegan pointed a finger at Tyler. "You need to go back out there! You have to look for them again!"

Michael jumped to his feet and got in Raegan's face. "No way!"

"Becca's right. He's the strongest swimmer of all of us," Raegan insisted. "Someone has to go out there!"

"I'm not going to let my best friend get killed," Michael said.

Each one raised their voice above the other's.

A loud whistle pierced the air, and everyone stopped to stare at Becca. "Everyone, shut up!"

"Don't tell us to shut up," Michael demanded. "We're trying to figure things out here."

"Well, shouting at each other isn't helping anything!"

"You're shouting," Milo pointed out. The twelve-year-old boy had been silent until now.

Becca shot him a glare but lowered her voice. "Tyler, what did you see inside the plane?"

"Nothing. Like I said, they weren't there."

"Their bodies?" Becca asked hesitantly.

Tyler shook his head. "Nothing."

Silence lingered as they let his words sink in.

"The plane is beached," Tyler continued. "Looks like it hit a sandbar." He pointed at the tail that protruded from the waves. Under the midday sun, the white metal was blinding. "I swam down through the cabin, but I couldn't get into the cockpit. I saw this bag on my way out." He gestured to Reagan's bloody arm. "Thought we might need it."

For the first time, Charlie noticed the red patch marked with a white cross and the words *First Aid*.

Charlie wished he had Tyler's strength to swim back out and help search. Sarah had been right to stop him. Charlie could barely hold up his own body, let alone swim out to the plane and back a second time. But Tyler was well conditioned for such a task. Back at the ranch, he spent countless hours in the pool. Even now, he hardly looked winded.

"Good call, Tyler," Michael said.

Tyler nodded.

"So …" Maxine tentatively spoke up again. "Are they dead?"

Milo shrugged. "Probably."

Maxine burst into tears. Sarah consoled her.

"Milo!" Becca scolded him. "We don't know that."

"So what do we do now?" Raegan asked. She sat in the sand beside the first-aid bag, dressing her wound.

A long pause followed.

"We go find help," Michael finally said. When he stood, Charlie noticed that his eyes had cleared. The fear was still there, but something had shifted in him.

"Absolutely not." Becca shook her head. "We need to stay right here on the beach. Surely, someone inland saw or heard the crash. Besides, there's a transponder on the plane. Someone will come for us. We need to be close to the plane when they do."

"What's a transponder?" Maxine asked.

"It's a device built into every aircraft," Kurtis said. The group turned to face him. His dark-brown skin and black curly hair glistened with beads of water. A small crack was visible on the left lens of his eyeglasses. He still clutched his watch. Charlie could see that he had taken it apart.

"It sends and receives radio signals," Kurtis said. "It can help someone locate us."

"Exactly," Becca chimed in. "Which is why we need to stay right here." She pointed to the sand at her feet.

Michael folded his arms across his chest. "That's fine. You can stay here then. I'm going to look for help. I'm not going to sit here and wait for rescue when some of us have injuries and the only two adults have disappeared."

"I'll go with you." Raegan raised her hand.

"I don't think it's a good idea for us to split up," Maxine said.

"It's not." Becca glared at Michael. "It's a terrible idea. We don't even know where we are."

"Exactly," Michael said. "We have no idea where we are, no clue what happened to Sister Cecile or the pilot, and we don't know why the plane crashed—or whether anyone even knows we did. I'm not waiting to find out. C'mon, Raegan. Tyler, are you coming?"

Tyler hesitated, then eyed Raegan. "She's right. I should swim back out and check for them again. Plus, I want to see if I can find my bag. We might be here awhile."

"That's stupid," Becca spat. "We're not going to be here long at all. You're lucky you didn't get yourself killed the first time you swam out there. Michael's right. What if the plane falls while you're in it? What if you get trapped inside?"

Tyler glanced back at the plane, then at Michael.

Michael shrugged. "Well, if you're going back out there, see if you can find my bag. And anything else that might be useful."

"You guys are idiots," Becca mumbled. She turned

her attention to Michael. "You're not really leaving, are you?"

He exchanged another look with Tyler, then said, "Yeah, and I'm leaving now. Anyone else coming?"

Charlie looked down and hoped no one would volunteer him to search for help.

He *would* go—if Michael weren't the leader of the expedition.

"I'll go," Milo said. He removed his shirt and began tying it around his head like a bandana.

Charlie saw Becca shoot him a curious stare then shake her head.

"Maybe we can make an SOS sign with some rocks," Sarah offered. "In case a plane flies over."

"I'm telling you; we don't need to do any of that," Becca said, her voice tinged with irritation. "They'll come looking for us. I'm certain someone already knows we've crashed. They can track the plane's transponder, and they're probably already on their way."

"You want to bet our lives on that?" Michael gave her a hard stare. "You want to bet *your* life on it?"

Becca didn't answer.

"That's what I thought."

Silence passed between the two of them.

Kurtis broke the tension. "This is just like that TV show *Lost*."

"Weren't there polar bears on the island in that show?" Milo asked. Everyone just stared at him. When he didn't get a response, he shrugged and jogged toward the forest. Michael and Raegan followed.

"We'll be back soon," Michael called over his shoulder.

Becca folded her arms over her chest, then shouted, "Be careful."

Charlie turned to Sarah. "I can help you with the sign."

"Me too," Maxine said. "I think it's a good idea."

Sarah offered a small smile to Charlie, then took the younger girl's hand. "Let's go find some rocks then."

Charlie followed.

"You guys are just wasting your energy." Becca called after them. "Someone is coming for us. I know it."

Charlie's wet socks rubbed against his shoes. He paused to slip them off and cast a glance back down the beach to see Tyler wade out toward the plane.

Charlie hoped Becca was right. This certainly wasn't the vacation he'd imagined. He laid out his socks and shoes to dry, then wiggled his toes in the sand. Yes, it was definitely not how he imagined it, but it was his first trip to the beach all the same. Besides, soon rescue would come for them. He might as well make the most of it.

Sweat beaded Charlie's brow and clung to his tight curls. He mopped his forehead and placed the last of his rocks into the outline of the letter *S* that Sarah had drawn in the sand. She'd suggested they scratch the letters into the sand before they lay the rocks, so they had a guide to follow. She always thought ahead like that.

Charlie was grateful she was here with him, though she hadn't talked much as they worked on the sign. Silence was a first for Sarah. Usually, she was outgoing and bubbly. But every time he'd glanced her way that afternoon, her lips formed a flat, tight line.

Charlie wiped his sweaty palms on his shorts and meandered back down the shore to where Tyler had dropped off several trips' worth of supplies. Exhausted, Charlie shielded his eyes from the sun, which now hung low over the water. Several hours had passed since Michael, Raegan, and Milo left.

Approximately fifty meters out from the shore, the setting sun cast the plane's tail in silhouette. Charlie guessed at the distance, knowing the swim was at least the length of the Olympic-size swimming pool back at the ranch. He couldn't believe Tyler had the strength and stamina to go back and forth that many times. Then again, that's what he did back home anyway.

Home.

The word struck Charlie with a strange sense of longing. But not for the ranch. Though he liked the estate—and Mr. Abbott—it had never felt like home. Not yet at least. Though his situation looked bleaker than ever, Charlie held on to the hope that the ranch would someday become his permanent residence. And that he'd soon safely return to it.

"Hey look. They're back." Sarah broke her silent streak and pulled Charlie from his thoughts. "C'mon. Let's see if they found help."

Maxine was close behind Sarah. Charlie quickened his pace and followed them.

Down the shore, Tyler lay back on the beach, his chest heaving. Sand clung to his hair and made it look even blonder than normal. He sat up only when Michael approached and nudged him in the ribs with his foot.

Becca, who had done nothing but sit in the surf the past several hours, finally stood. Raegan and Milo, who were a few paces behind Michael, finally joined them. Milo's shirt was no longer on his head. Now it swung from one of his arms as a makeshift sling filled with bananas.

"Well?" Becca asked.

"We have good news and bad news," Milo said.

Becca rolled her eyes. "Just spit it out."

"Which do you want first?"

She glared at Milo. "The good news."

"The good news is we found bananas." Milo held up his T-shirt.

"The bad news is there's no one on this island," Michael interjected.

"Wait, we're on an island?"

"What do you mean there's no one on the island?" Charlie asked.

Michael narrowed his eyes at him. "What do you think it means? *We're alone.* Stranded, in fact. No people, no civilization."

"That's not possible," Becca said. Fear tinted her voice. "Maybe they're just farther inland. You didn't walk far enough."

"You're not listening to me." Michael's words came out clipped. "We're on an island. We know because we walked the entire thing. It's not big."

"Yeah," Raegan chimed in. "Maybe about a mile to a mile-and-a-half long. Close to the same distance across."

"Okay, so—wait." Becca rubbed her temples. "Then what island would this be?"

"None that I know of." Kurtis spoke up. He adjusted his broken glasses on his nose. "In fact, I have some concerns about our location." Charlie had noticed him scouting the beach earlier in the day while the others were gone.

"I think we all have some concerns, dude." Milo shifted his T-shirt full of bananas.

"Go on, Kurtis," Becca said.

"Well, as I prepared for our trip, I studied the map of our flight path and the areas surrounding our destination."

"No surprises there," Michael mumbled.

Kurtis didn't acknowledge the comment. "Your description of the island doesn't match anything along the route or anywhere near Cozumel."

"C'mon, Kurtis," Michael said. "Do you really know *all* the islands near Cozumel?"

"Of course not. But that's not the only thing that's concerning to me."

"What else?"

"Well, have you noticed the water? It's murky."

"Murky?" Sarah said.

"Yeah." Kurtis pointed to the ocean. "The water should be bright blue, turquoise even. And crystal clear."

"He's right." Milo nodded. "I looked up pictures on Google before we left."

Charlie started to speak but hesitated when he saw Michael look his way. He decided to ignore him. "That's what the water looked like shortly before we crashed," Charlie said. "I saw it out the window of the plane."

"Yes, I noticed that too," Kurtis said. "But if we're in the Gulf of Mexico—which is where we should be— then we should see clear-blue water here, even from the beach."

Charlie peered out at the waves. He'd noticed the brownish-green sea earlier and had even wondered how Tyler could see anything underwater while in the plane.

Kurtis continued. "I also haven't seen or heard a single bird since we've been here. And there doesn't seem to be any insects either. It's all very odd."

Michael fixed his eyes on Charlie. "Does that sound right, Chucky? No insects? Not even any invisible, glowing butterflies?"

"Shut up, Michael," Sarah said.

Michael shrugged.

Charlie kept ignoring him.

"So what does that mean?" Becca asked, pulling them back on topic.

"It means"—Tyler finally stood to join them—"it's a good thing I got some of our stuff off the plane. Looks like we might be here a while." He shot a glare at Becca.

"Yeah, Becca," Michael chimed in. "Where's the rescue you promised? Any planes fly over while we were gone?"

"Not yet," Joey, one of the youngest boys in the group, said quietly. He'd been silent since they'd crashed.

"This really is like *Lost*," Milo said to himself, then added, "Cool."

"I'm scared." Maxine reached for Sarah's hand.

Charlie hated to admit it, but so was he.

When he caught Sarah's eye, though, he stuffed his own angst down as far as he could. Sarah had been strong for him when he was nervous about the plane ride. Now, it was time for him to be strong for her. He wouldn't mention to her that his fears about the plane were warranted.

Charlie cleared his throat and avoided looking at Michael as he spoke. "We should set up a spot to sleep," he said. "We can use these tarps." He pointed to the tarps Tyler had brought to shore.

"That's a great idea, Charlie," Sarah said.

"Yeah," he heard Michael say and felt the boy's eyes on him. "Great idea, Charlie." Sarcasm dripped from his words.

"We still have the transponder," Becca said. "Someone will find us. I know it."

"Look!" Raegan said excitedly. "There's an inflatable raft in this emergency pack." She was digging through one of the bags Tyler had brought back from the plane. "We can use it to find rescue or civilization!"

"Are you crazy?" Becca asked. "Do you even know

what terrible things can happen to us out on the open water? Dehydration, starvation …" She started ticking off the reasons on her fingers.

"Sharks," Milo added.

Becca nodded. "Exactly, sharks. No—we stay with the plane and the transponder. The raft should be a last resort. Someone *will* find us if we stay put."

Sarah glanced at Charlie, then back at Becca. "I hope you're right."

"Whatever." Tyler shrugged. "In the meantime, I'm hungry." He pulled out several granola bars from one of the bags he'd brought to shore. "Might be a little wet, but it's still food." He tossed one to Maxine but no one else. Charlie had noticed that Tyler had a soft spot for the young girl, despite being unkind to everyone else.

"Don't forget the bananas." Milo plopped his T-shirt down in the center of the group.

Charlie saw Becca clench her jaw. "You guys are acting like we're camping."

Michael tore open a granola bar and ripped off a bite with his teeth. "It was Charlie's idea," he said through a mouthful. "You said it yourself, Becca: someone is coming for us." His eyes found Charlie's. "We shouldn't panic." He grabbed a tarp, stood, and marched by, slamming his shoulder into Charlie's.

"We can set up camp over here," Michael called

out, pointing toward the forest. He walked to a point halfway between the water's edge and the vegetation. "Don't want the high tide to soak us in our sleep."

Sarah released Maxine's hand and stepped away from the group. She motioned for Charlie to follow. When they were several yards away, she lowered her voice and said, "I have a bad feeling about this."

"Me too," Charlie whispered.

"It's like they're drawing sides."

Charlie nodded. "I noticed."

Sarah clutched her hands together in front of her. The white shirt she wore was untucked from her skort. Dirt from the rocks stained the once pristine white fabric. Her normal air of confidence was gone. "Are we on a side?" she asked.

Charlie heard the hesitancy in his friend's voice. "We *are* on a side," he said. "We're on each other's side. No matter what happens, you and I will stick together." Then he remembered the words she spoke to him earlier that day in the library. "I've got your back, Sarah," he said with a smile. "I know we're not family yet, but that's what friends do."

"Thank you," she whispered. A genuine smile appeared on his best friend's face, and for a brief second, Charlie felt not just hopeful but confident and strong.

It was short-lived, though. Because up the beach,

visible in the quickly fading sunlight, Charlie saw Michael spread a tarp over the sand. He stared at Charlie. Even at this distance, Charlie could read Michael's expression, and it said that nothing had changed between the two them. If anything, Charlie guessed, things were about to get worse.

CHAPTER FOUR

PERSPIRATION DRIPPED down Charlie's forehead and ran into his eyes. He stopped for the second time to wipe the stinging sweat from his face. It was around one o'clock in the afternoon—or so Kurtis had said—and the island's tropical heat was worse than anything Charlie had ever experienced.

Fourteen-year-old Kurtis marched ahead of Charlie through the dense growth, seemingly unaffected by the sweltering humidity. The boy casually wiped his brow, then glanced at the watch on his wrist. It was the only piece of technology the kids had that still worked. Their iPhones had been lost in the crash, drained of battery, or rendered useless by the complete lack of signal on the island.

"How'd you know how to fix your watch?" Charlie had asked Kurtis earlier that morning.

He'd shrugged. "Simple. I built it."

Charlie hadn't been surprised. Back at the ranch, he'd seen Kurtis assemble and launch small rockets from the field at dusk. It wasn't a stretch to believe he could build his own watch.

Charlie adjusted the thin strap of the overstuffed duffle bag on his shoulder. It must have weighed close to thirty pounds—and all of it mangos.

Charlie still wasn't sure how Sarah had convinced him to go into the forest with Michael and his crew to collect food while she remained on the beach with Becca, Maxine, and Joey. But here he was. And lugging the largest and heaviest of the bags.

Charlie heard Raegan laugh at something Tyler had said to her. The two of them hiked ahead of Kurtis, each of them wearing a sensibly weighted backpack filled with bananas and papayas. Kurtis had emptied the first-aid bag that morning and now used it to carry his haul. And wandering somewhere in the nearby brush, Milo sported his T-shirt fruit sling loaded with bananas.

Of course, Michael had given Charlie the duffle—the heaviest and most awkward of the bags to carry. A mark already formed on his shoulder where the straps had dug into his skin. Charlie tried to shift it to a more comfortable position, but it didn't help. He glared at the back of Michael's head, wishing he were on the beach with Sarah.

That morning, Michael had quickly asserted himself as the leader of their expedition. Now, marching at the front of their group, he carried nothing but a long stick, swatting vines and vegetation like an explorer with a machete. The stick wasn't doing much to clear the trail, but Charlie wasn't about to tell Michael that. Not after the way Michael had harassed him while picking fruit. Tyler had jumped in on the bullying as well, teasing Charlie about having to climb a mango tree because he couldn't reach the fruit from the ground.

Charlie rolled his shoulders and tried to shrug off their comments—and the unbearable weight of the bag—but it was becoming harder to ignore Michael's bullying. Charlie's patience was thin. He wasn't sure how much longer he could peaceably put up with Michael.

Or the dreadful heat.

He hoisted the bag and followed the other children.

"Hey, Kurtis?" Charlie called up to him. "Do you think a rescue plane flew by while we've been out?"

Kurtis glanced over his shoulder and shook his head. "As small as the island is, we would've heard a plane if there was one."

"A boat then," Charlie said, trying to remain optimistic.

Kurtis didn't respond.

It had been close to twenty-four hours since the

trauma of the plane crash, and there was still no sign of rescue or of Sister Cecile or the pilot. Their disappearance unnerved Charlie.

He stopped again to shift the strap. This time, he switched the bag to his other shoulder. His stomach gurgled with a hollow and painful growl. The only thing he'd eaten since the plane meal yesterday was a granola bar, which he split with Sarah, and a slightly green banana from Milo's haul the night before.

Charlie had tried to eat one of the mangos they found that morning, but Michael slapped it out of his hand.

"We need to wait and eat with the whole group," he'd said.

Yet Charlie was fairly sure he'd seen both Tyler and Michael chewing something as they'd hiked.

Charlie paused and reached into his pocket for the water bottle he'd stuffed there. Tyler had thought to bring several bottles to shore. They'd even found a freshwater spring on their hike that morning where they could refill them.

The water dampened Charlie's hunger, and he returned the bottle to his pocket. When he picked up his feet to continue, a low vine snagged on his shoe. Charlie tried to yank it free, but the weight of the bag threw him off balance. He thrust his hands out to catch himself and broke his fall on a sticker bush. The burn of the tiny thorns flared across his skin.

Kurtis stopped, then shouted to the rest of the group ahead of them. "Hey guys, wait up. Charlie fell."

Charlie pushed himself to his feet. Thin red lines of blood formed on his palms. He clenched his jaw and swung the duffle bag off his shoulder. It thudded against the ground.

"Hey! Watch it," Michael said, approaching him. "You're going to bruise the mangos."

A now familiar heat rose within Charlie. He glared at Michael but said nothing.

Michael stared back. "You need to be more careful, Chucky. You can get away with being completely useless back home, but we need you to pull your weight around here."

Charlie balled his hands into fists. "I *am* pulling my weight. I'm pulling more weight than anyone else."

Michael cocked his head to the side and took a step closer. "Want to run that by me again, Chucky?"

"You gave me the heaviest bag," Charlie said. "And you're not even carrying anything."

A smirk formed on Michael's lips. "You know what, you're right. That was my bad." Michael yanked the duffle from Charlie. "What was I thinking, counting on you to carry such a heavy bag? You're the smallest one here. I should've known you'd be too weak." Michael shouldered the bag. "I'll carry it."

"No," Charlie said with defiance.

"No?"

"I can carry it," Charlie peered down at his sliced palms. "I just need a minute. Can we take a break?"

"We don't have time for a break," Kurtis said. He glanced at his watch. "We've already been gone an hour longer than we said we would, and we still have at least another hour's hike back to the beach. We need to keep moving."

Raegan pointed to the duffle. "Give it here. I'll carry it, so we can keep moving."

"Now hold on a second," Michael said in a mocking tone. "Charlie said he can carry it. He just needs a little break, that's all. Don't we all need a little break?"

Raegan glared at Charlie. "No."

Kurtis shrugged. "I'm fine to keep going."

"Me too." Milo said, appearing from the bushes. He hadn't stuck to the main path the entire day but always seemed to be close enough to know exactly what was happening.

Charlie wiped the blood from his palms onto his shorts. The scrapes weren't deep. "I'm fine." He held out his hand to Michael. "Give it back."

Michael started to hand him the duffle, then said,

"I've got an idea." He turned to Raegan. "Why don't you, Kurtis, and Milo go on ahead of us. Tyler and I will stay here with Charlie a minute while he catches his breath."

"I don't need to catch my breath." Charlie said through gritted teeth.

"Of course you do," Michael said. "And Tyler and I will wait for you."

"Is splitting up a good idea?" Kurtis asked.

Raegan rolled her eyes. "It'll be fine. Let's go."

"Yeah," Michael said with a grin. "It'll be fine. You guys head back to the beach. We'll be right behind you."

A pit formed in Charlie's stomach. And despite the heat, a chill snaked up the back of his neck.

"Let's go, Milo," Raegan called over her shoulder. She was already several yards down the trail. "Kurtis, c'mon."

Kurtis met Charlie's stare. He hesitated a moment, then turned to follow Raegan and Milo. Once they were out of sight, Michael said to Charlie, "C'mon. There's a spot to sit up here." He turned, and Tyler followed.

Charlie hoisted the duffle bag, unease now coursing through his body.

He followed Michael and Tyler through the dense foliage to a small clearing, where a narrow plateau ended in a steep drop.

Michael and Tyler took a seat and dangled their

feet over the edge. Between them they set the bag Tyler had been carrying. Michael unzipped it and offered a banana to Tyler, then peeled one for himself. Heat filled Charlie's cheeks.

Michael turned to look over his shoulder. "C'mon, Chucky." He patted the space beside him. "Come have a seat and take a break. Want a banana?" He grinned.

Charlie slid the duffle bag strap off his shoulder. He set the bag down, carefully this time, but didn't move toward Michael and Tyler. To the right of the two boys, a thin path zigzagged down the rocky cliffside. Charlie, terrified when they'd climbed it earlier that day, did his best not to peer over the edge. About twenty feet below, the ocean crashed against craggy boulders. Any anxiety he'd conquered during the first half of their plane ride returned, along with a paralyzing and dizzying fear of heights. Already, Charlie dreaded their descent. He noted the way Michael and Tyler had positioned themselves so Charlie would have to walk right past them to get to the trail.

"No thanks," Charlie said. "I'll just sit back here." His stomach growled.

"Sure you don't want a banana? Here." Michael held it out toward him.

Charlie bit the inside of his lip. There was no way he was going anywhere near those boys, not when they were the only thing standing between Charlie and the edge. "No. I'm okay," Charlie said.

"I think he's scared," Tyler said.

"Of the cliff?" Michael asked Tyler. He turned to face Charlie. "Or of us?" He let out a low laugh. "Either way, I'd say this is the perfect time to overcome your fear. What do you say, Chucky?"

Charlie glanced past Michael's shoulder to where the ocean met the sky. He heard the crash of the waves below. "No."

"C'mon, Chucky. I know you're a wimp, but really? You won't even come near the edge?"

Charlie clenched his teeth. "I'm not a wimp."

"My bad," Michael said. "You're a chicken."

Tyler stood, stuck his thumbs under his armpits, and flapped his arms like wings while making a clucking sound.

"You guys are jerks," Charlie said under his breath. He turned away from them.

"What was that?" Michael asked.

"Nothing," Charlie muttered.

Michael jabbed Tyler with a finger. "Hear that, Ty? He can't even call us jerks to our faces."

"'Cuz he's too chicken," Tyler added.

Charlie balled his hands into fists and turned. He started to shout at them, to tell Michael and Tyler what he really thought. But he couldn't.

Michael raised his eyebrows and waited. "What?

You have something to say to me?"

Charlie forced his shoulders to relax, but the tension in his jaw remained. "You don't know me," Charlie said.

"Really?" Michael asked. "So you're saying you're not a totally useless wimp who's afraid of everything?"

Charlie just stared back at him.

"Then prove it," Michael said. "Prove to me you're not everything I think you are."

Charlie didn't move.

"He'll never do it," Tyler said.

"Of course, he won't," Michael said. "Because he's a chicken."

Michael and Tyler dissolved into laughter.

Before Charlie could stop himself, he shouted, "If I do it, will you stop bullying me?"

Michael and Tyler fell silent. They stared at Charlie.

"If I do it, will you stop bullying me?" Charlie repeated, already regretting that he'd asked. This was a terrible idea.

Michael and Tyler exchanged glances. Michael shrugged, then looked to Charlie. "Sure, Charlie. Come stand on the edge of this cliff. Prove that you're not scared, and we'll stop bullying you."

Charlie shifted on his feet. It was the first time Michael had called him Charlie instead of Chucky.

"Really?" Charlie asked. He took a step closer.

Michael smirked. "Sure."

Charlie backed away. "Never mind," he said.

Leaving the bag of mangos, Charlie turned and started back the way they'd come. He'd find another way down to the beach—at least, he hoped he could.

Tyler quickly moved in front of him and blocked his path. He grabbed Charlie by the shoulders and spun him around.

"I don't think so, Charlie," Tyler said. "If you leave now, that will be the ultimate chicken move." Tyler pushed Charlie in Michael's direction.

Charlie tried shrugging the older boy's hands off his shoulders, but Tyler was a head taller than him and much stronger.

"Look," Michael said. "I'll be honest with you. I'm getting sick of the bullying too."

Charlie stared at Michael, trying to read beyond his words. "What do you mean?" Charlie asked.

Michael flinched. "Don't get me wrong; I've had fun pushing you around, but you're the most annoying person I've ever met," he said with a sneer. "No matter how hard I push, you just take it. Seriously, Charlie. Doesn't anything get under your skin? Don't you have any self-respect?"

His words hit harder than anything Michael had ever said to Charlie.

Did Charlie have any self-respect?

"You'll stop then?" Charlie asked. A voice in his head screamed that this was a terrible idea, but he heard himself say, "You'll stop teasing me?" Charlie searched Michael's face. "Say it. Say you'll stop bullying me."

"I'm not going to say it," Michael said. "You're just going to have to trust me."

Charlie huffed. "I'm out of here." This time he managed to shrug Tyler off his shoulders. He stormed toward the trees.

"Charlie!" Michael called after him. "If you walk away from me now, I'll make your life miserable."

Charlie stopped and turned.

"You thought things were bad before?" Michael shook his head. "You have no idea how bad things can get."

Charlie stared at him.

"Trust me," Michael said. "Come stand on the edge of this cliff for ten seconds. Prove that you're not a useless coward." He waited for Charlie's response.

The rhythmic crash of the waves below punctuated the boys' silence.

Charlie looked at the forest, then back at the cliff. He sighed and walked toward Michael, regretting his decision with every step.

Michael and Tyler stepped aside and made space for Charlie between them at the ledge. When he inched his toes to the lip, a pebble tumbled over the side. Dizziness overwhelmed him as he watched the small rock disappear. Charlie swallowed.

A hand clamped down on each of his thin shoulders.

"Hey! What are you doing?" Charlie demanded.

"I said you have to trust me, didn't I?" Michael said. "This is like a reverse trust fall. Tyler and I will each have a hand on you the whole time."

Charlie swallowed. This was the worst decision of his life. But now, there was nowhere to go.

Michael and Tyler gripped him tighter.

"Ready?" Michael asked.

No. Everything inside Charlie screamed no.

"Ten seconds?" he said aloud.

"Ten seconds," Michael confirmed.

Charlie's eyes drifted down then darted back up.

"I'll count," Michael said. "Ten, nine, eight, seven …"

Charlie's eyes focused on the horizon. He didn't dare look down again. Perspiration beaded on his forehead, and this time, it wasn't from the heat.

"Six, five, four …"

Charlie tried to focus on anything but the faintness that flooded his body. He even tried to shift his attention to the slight burn that lingered on his scraped palms.

Michael's face was in his periphery, unnerved.

Three more seconds. Charlie coached himself. He could do this.

"Threeee."

Michael drew out the word.

"Twooo …"

There was a smile in Michael's voice.

"Now!" he shouted.

The pressure of Michael's and Tyler's grips shifted. The boys thrust their weight against Charlie's shoulders and pushed him over the edge.

Images from the plane crash flashed in Charlie's memory.

Panic filled his mind.

Jolts of anxiety pulsed under his skin.

But just as quickly as the fall began, it halted.

Charlie jerked to a stop, his shoulders still held by Michael and Tyler, his body dangling above the white-capped ocean waves.

The boys yanked his arms hard and pulled him back onto the cliff. Charlie fell to the ground, landing on his back. Arms outspread, he gripped the earth. Michael and Tyler doubled over with laughter, delighted with their horrible prank.

Michael was right. Charlie had no self-respect. If he had, he never would have put himself in this position. His self-loathing collided with every other emotion Charlie had felt over the past three months: the confusion he'd first felt toward Michael, then the envy, the judgment, the anger, and now, the hatred.

Charlie gritted his teeth, jumped to his feet, and barreled into Michael. Caught off guard, the boy stumbled backward toward the cliff's edge, but caught himself.

Michael's smile and laughter faded.

"You're going to regret that, Chucky." He straightened his shoulders. "You know, I never could put my finger on it, but since the day I met you, I knew you didn't belong with us. You don't have what it takes to be in the Abbott family—or any family, for that matter." Michael's lips curled into a sneer. "That's probably why your parents abandoned you."

Something snapped in Charlie's mind. He didn't stop to think, just reacted. He rushed Michael with outstretched hands and shoved him with a strength he didn't know he had.

A sound somewhere between a scream and cry slipped from Michael's lips.

And then he was gone.

Tyler rushed to the ledge.

Charlie stumbled backward.

He'd shoved Michael over the cliff.

Seconds stretched like an eternity, then he heard, "Help!"

Charlie ran to the ledge and peered over.

Michael had caught himself on a rock, and Tyler already had a hand extended to him.

"Grab my arm!" Tyler shouted. "I'll pull you up."

Charlie turned and paced away, unable to watch as Tyler helped Michael to safety.

Charlie's mind whirled as he gripped his hair. What had he done? He'd nearly killed Michael.

"Charlie!"

It was Michael's voice.

Charlie turned.

Michael stood beside Tyler. Scrapes lined his left arm and cheek. His face was ashen, eyes wild with fury. A scream poured from Michael's mouth and echoed against the cliffside. He sprinted at Charlie and crashed into him. Charlie sprawled on the ground, but before he could get up, Michael was on top of him, his fist pulled back.

He landed the punch.

Pain blossomed on Charlie's face. The taste of metal filled his mouth. Warm liquid pooled in the corners of his lips.

"Okay, Michael, stop," Tyler said, his voice even.

Michael hit Charlie again, this time harder.

"C'mon, Michael," Tyler repeated. "That's enough."

Rage filled Michael eyes, and Charlie knew he wasn't going to stop.

"Michael!" Tyler tried to pull him off Charlie, but Michael shoved him away.

"Get off me!" Michael shouted. "Get off me, Ty!" Michael pulled his fist back again.

Tyler caught his arm. "That's enough. You're hurting him!"

Michael struggled against Tyler's grip. "I know!"

Finally, Tyler managed to pull Michael off.

On the ground, Charlie wiped his mouth with his forearm. Blood smeared his brown skin. Pain pulsed in his face. He glanced at Michael. Rage filled the boy's eyes.

Michael shoved Tyler away and closed the gap between him and Charlie. He dropped to his knees and lowered his face until he was a breath away.

"Back home, I just wanted to keep you out of my family," Michael growled.

Charlie could smell the banana on his breath.

"And now, this island is going to help me do just that." Michael shoved a finger in Charlie's face. "The rest of us are going to get rescued and go back home to Mr. Abbott. But you?" Michael shook his head, then stood. "I'm going to make sure you never make it off this island."

Several paces ahead of Charlie, Michael and Tyler burst through the tree line and onto the beach. The rest of their group sprawled on the tarps they'd slept on the night before, eating the fruit Raegan and Kurtis had brought. Nearby, Milo had built a sandcastle and was affixing rocks to the structure.

Tyler dropped his backpack, and Michael threw down the duffle bag he'd taken from Charlie.

"What took you guys so long?" Raegan asked.

Charlie lingered near the forest before spotting Sarah. He shuffled through the sand toward the group, head down.

Tyler wiped his brow and glared at Raegan. "Charlie tried to kill Michael, that's what took us so long."

"What?"

Nine pairs of eyes pinned Charlie with their stares.

"No," Charlie said. "That's not what happened."

Sarah rose to her feet. "Charlie?"

"Yeah," Tyler said. "He shoved Michael off a cliff!"

"Charlie!" Becca exclaimed.

Raegan narrowed her eyes. "What is wrong with you?" she demanded.

Maxine approached Michael. "Are you okay?"

Michael huffed. "I'm fine."

Rage filled Charlie. A light touch landed on his forearm, and he instinctively shoved it away.

It was Sarah. Confusion marked her face. "Charlie, is that true? You pushed Michael off a cliff?" Her eyes landed on his busted lip. She touched his arm again.

"Michael's lucky to be alive," Tyler said. "No thanks to Charlie."

Charlie pushed Sarah's hand away again. His insides boiled. "They're not telling you the whole truth! If you would all just listen, I can tell you what really happened."

"What really happened," Michael interjected, "is that Charlie tried to kill me."

Charlie shot him with a stare. "That's not the whole story."

"You're right." Michael stormed toward Charlie, fists at his sides. "The rest of the story is that now I'm going to kill you!" Michael lunged and shoved Charlie into the sand.

"Guys! Stop!" Becca shouted.

Before Michael could attack again, Tyler had him pinned.

Sarah helped Charlie to his feet. Her fingers gripped his. "Charlie, how could you?"

"How could I?" Charlie threw his hands into the air. "Of course you're going to side with Michael. Everyone always does."

He stormed down the beach, away from the accusations.

"Charlie, wait!"

He heard Sarah call after him but quickened his pace. The torrent of emotions electrified his body. His skin hot with rage.

"Slow down," she panted. "Charlie, stop!"

"What?"

"Just talk to me for a second!"

He stopped and turned.

It took Sarah a few seconds to catch up. "What happened out there?" she asked.

Charlie crossed his arms over his chest. "Why? You're not going to believe me anyway."

Sarah tilted her head. "What's going on with you? You're acting crazy."

"*I'm acting crazy?*" Charlie shook his head. "No. What's crazy is that Michael and all his friends have been bullying me since the day I walked onto the ranch, and now suddenly I'm the bad guy."

She lowered her voice. "Tell me what happened."

"What happened is what always happens!" Charlie shouted. "Michael is a monster. I hate him."

"So you pushed him off a cliff?"

Charlie spun on Sarah. "I snapped, okay! I'm so tired of this. I'm tired of him!"

Sarah just stared at Charlie.

He sighed, then tried to recall the events. "I don't know how it happened exactly, but I shoved Michael." Silence lingered between them. "And he went over the edge. He caught himself, though," Charlie quickly added. "And Tyler helped him up."

Charlie could tell that Sarah was trying to keep herself composed by the way she shifted her shoulders back and took a deep breath before speaking.

"I mean, it was an accident, though, right?" she asked. "We can settle this with the group. You didn't shove him on purpose?"

"No," Charlie insisted. "I mean—yes—but—you weren't there, Sarah!"

Pressure mounted in Charlie's head. Tears prickled behind his eyes as he remembered Michael's hateful comment.

The remark that broke him.

That's probably why your parents abandoned you.

"They were cruel to me, Sarah. Absolutely cruel."

"Yes, but"—Sarah lowered her tone—"Charlie, you could have killed him. You're lucky Tyler was there to help—"

"*I'm lucky?*" Charlie spit out a laugh. "No." He jabbed a finger in Sarah's face. "I am *not* lucky. I'm cursed, Sarah. Everywhere I go, no matter what I do, I'm hated by everyone. *Everyone!*" he shouted. The flare of emotions continued to rage within him. He lowered his voice. "Even you."

Sarah shook her head. "Charlie, I don't hate you. Where's this coming from?"

Charlie shoved his hands into his pockets. "You said you had my back, Sarah. Remember? You said, 'That's what friends do.'" He waited for her to say something, but she didn't. He shrugged. "Looks like family is more important than friendship."

Charlie turned.

"Charlie, stop! Where are you going?"

"Away."

"Away to where?"

"To be alone," he spat. "Which is exactly what I deserve."

"What happened to us being on each other's side?" she asked. "No matter what?"

Charlie stopped and turned. "You tell me. You're the one who chose Michael's side."

"Charlie! I'm not choosing his side; I'm trying to help you."

"Oh really? You're helping me? Is that what you're

doing?" Charlie closed the gap between them. "Funny, I used to believe you when you said things like that."

"Oh, so you don't believe me anymore then, huh?"

"I only believe *real* friends." As soon as Charlie said it, he regretted it.

The look of hurt that crossed Sarah's face was worse than anything he could have imagined. "Fine. Go on then," she spat. "See how you do on your own without any friends. Because you don't have any now! Not a single one!"

Charlie turned and didn't look back because, this time, he believed her.

Chapter Five

A BLANKET OF MIDNIGHT BLUE filled Charlie's field of vision. Bright specs of light dotted the night sky's surface and taunted him with their brilliance. Even the moon seemed too bright for his sour mood.

Charlie had kept his distance from Sarah and the other kids for the remainder of the day. The looks they'd given him were enough to remind him that, though he was with them in their terrifying circumstances, Charlie would never be a part of their family.

Leaning up on his shoulder, he glanced over at the girls' tarp a few yards away. Sarah slept; Maxine snuggled up beside her. Down the beach, the fire Milo had built faded to embers, but a few of the children's silhouettes lingered around its glow.

Charlie rolled to his side in his spot on the farthest edge of the boys' tarp and pulled a corner over his legs. The island was cool at night—one reason he couldn't sleep. But the main reason was the torrent of emotion that swirled inside him. Waves of anxiety washed over him followed by pure rage. He focused on his breathing and tried to settle his mind, but it didn't help.

Several minutes later Charlie sensed other boys settling onto the tarp for sleep, but Charlie didn't acknowledge them. Instead, he kept his eyes fixed on the darkened rainforest fifteen yards from where he lay. Eventually, the soft sounds of measured breathing came from behind him, and he knew the others had fallen asleep.

Charlie's eyes searched the darkness, his thoughts becoming stranger as sleep came to steal him away. A weight settled on his eyelids, and a heaviness filled his chest. His own breathing slowed. The sound of his inhale and exhale synchronized with the pull of the waves that beat the shoreline behind him. He blinked, his eyes lingering closed before reopening.

From somewhere in the distance of the nighttime forest, or perhaps manifested from a dream, a soft glow fluttered toward Charlie. Like a star come to life, the subtle light approached and settled on a rock not five feet from his face. Charlie's tired eyes blinked the image into focus.

The butterfly.

Charlie propped himself up on one elbow and

leaned forward, his mind now fully awake. He squinted. The creature's wings pulsed open and closed. The soft yellow glow filled its body and spread to the tips of its wings. The light was so subtle, a casual observer might not be sure if it came from the moon or an interior luminance.

But Charlie knew.

This butterfly glowed.

He rolled onto his belly, doing his best to not rustle the tarp, then pulled himself into the sand and inched closer. The butterfly didn't seem bothered by Charlie's presence, not even when he lowered his face six inches from its wings.

He'd never gotten this close to one before. It looked so real.

Charlie hesitated, then reached a tentative hand toward it.

The butterfly fluttered up from the rock and hovered above him. He rolled onto his back to watch it.

That's when Charlie remembered that Kurtis had said there were no insects on the island.

Even earlier that day, when Charlie and the other kids went in search of food, the forest had been silent, not filled with an ambient buzz.

Other than the children from the plane, this butterfly was the first sign of life Charlie had seen on the island.

But it was probably just another one of his weird hallucinations.

His eyes followed the glowing creature as it fluttered. It was striking against the stary backdrop, like a living constellation. Its body drifted lower. Charlie reached a sleepy hand toward it. The butterfly came to rest on his fingertip, and shock overwhelmed him.

It was real.

Charlie brought his hand toward his face and flattened his palm. The butterfly crawled across the back of his hand and turned as if facing him. It tapped its tiny feet and pulsed its wings once, twice, then three times. Then it fluttered away and landed on the rock where Charlie had first seen it.

He rose to his feet and stepped closer. The butterfly lifted into the sky again, then settled onto another rock, this time nearer to the tree line.

Charlie followed.

Again, the butterfly took to the air, but this time, it came to rest on the trunk of a tree at the edge of the forest.

Charlie approached, and the butterfly seemed to wait for him.

When Charlie reached it, the insect took off again and disappeared into the thick undergrowth.

Charlie watched it go until it was merely a speck in

the distance. He took a cautious step, careful to not to make a sound, then cast a glance back at the darkened shoreline and the tarps where the other children slept.

He could just make out Sarah's form in the moonlight. An image of her face filled his mind—the look she'd given Charlie when she'd told him he no longer had any friends.

Charlie turned back to the forest. He could barely see the butterfly now. Soon it would be gone.

Just like Sarah.

Just like everyone else he'd ever tried to befriend.

And in that moment, Charlie knew he had no one.

But there was something else he knew now too.

He wasn't crazy.

And the butterfly was real.

Charlie pushed every other thought from his head and stepped into the forest.

Down the shoreline, past the long-dead fire, Michael sat in the sand, knees drawn to his chest. He flicked a blade in his pocketknife open and closed, then open again. His eyes stared at the black ocean waves. Silver outlines marked their crests as they raced to shore, the moonlight glimmering on their surface. He couldn't sleep. Didn't even try. Because every time he closed his eyes, whether seated or standing, Michael could see the world flip, feel the plummeting sensation of the fall, hear the sound of his own terror slip from his lips. He gritted his teeth, hating that Charlie—of all people, *Charlie*—could strike so much terror within him.

He hated the boy now more than ever.

Michael remembered the day he first saw Charlie, across the archery field back at the ranch. He'd learned that morning a new kid would be joining them at Saint Francis's Boys and Girls Home. What Michael didn't know was that it would be a boy his age. Someone Mr. Abbott found intriguing enough to break his own rules.

Charlie was different.

Michael remembered the way Mr. Abbott had draped an arm around the boy's shoulder as he led him past the stable. Remembered the sound of Mr. Abbott's laughter when the boy made a joke. Back then, Michael couldn't figure out why Charlie had filled him with such disdain. Even up until earlier that day, Michael still couldn't put his finger on it. But now, it didn't matter. Michael despised Charlie.

Even more, he hated that Charlie was the reason falling asleep terrified him. If his lids closed, surely he'd see his life flash before his eyes—not just in the plane crash, but in his near plummet from the cliff.

Michael saw movement out of the corner of his eye. He flicked the knife closed and watched as one of the other kids rose from the sleeping area and made their way up the beach toward the forest. Moonlight outlined the familiar figure.

"Speak of the devil," Michael whispered.

He watched as Charlie hovered near the tree line, glanced back at the beach, then slipped into the trees.

Michael stood and dusted the sand from his shorts. He flicked his pocketknife open once again.

"This is going to be too easy," he said, then followed Charlie into the forest.

It took Michael several minutes to catch up without giving away his position. He kept his distance while maintaining sight of Charlie, though it was tough in the dark. But Charlie was moving slow, stopping every so often as if searching for something before continuing.

What's he doing? Michael pushed through the thick underbrush.

But he didn't spend much thought on why Charlie had entered the forest.

Only on how Michael would ensure he'd never make it out.

A rock snagged Michael's foot. He stumbled, and pain flared across his hand. The blade of his pocketknife slipped through the meat of his right hand. Michael bit his lip and inhaled hard, silencing his scream. Hot liquid pooled in his palm, and he knew the cut was deep. He could feel his pulse throb.

He managed to close the blade, now sticky with his blood. After returning it to his pocket, he ripped his right sleeve off his shirt and wrapped the cloth around his hand. He could just barely see Charlie.

Pain intensified Michael's hatred for the boy he now stalked. Flooded with a rage more intense than ever, Michael clenched his jaw and followed Charlie.

The butterfly drifted a few feet ahead of Charlie and led him into a crescent-shaped clearing. Moonlight cast a silvery glow across the open space. A rocky cliffside jutted from the earth at the far end of the field where a tree, blacker than the night sky, grew from the soil. Gnarled, leafless branches sprawled across the cliff's surface, mirroring the overgrown root system that sprang from the earth. The butterfly flew toward it. Charlie stifled a shiver, then followed.

The tree loomed over him as he approached, some of the branches drooping so low Charlie had to duck beneath them. He'd never seen anything like it. A strange feeling overwhelmed him as he approached, and the closer he got, the more intense the feeling became. A sense of dread and excitement mingled in his belly. The air seemed to hum. Charlie felt drawn to the tree, and at the same time, he wanted to run from it. He paused a moment beneath the branches, then decided to continue.

He followed the butterfly around the side of the tree. It landed on the face of the cliff. This close, Charlie could see that the trunk touched the rock, almost as if the two were one.

The glowing butterfly pulsed its wings where it rested, and Charlie took a step closer. This time the creature didn't move. It seemed their journey together was over, as if this was the place the butterfly had been leading him all along.

Charlie reached for the insect, daring to touch its shimmering wings. A velvety fuzz covered them. He placed a hand in front of it, hoping it would crawl onto his fingers again. He rested the palm of his hand against the cool stone surface and waited.

The rock groaned.

Charlie jumped back.

A door not much larger than his body opened on the cliffside. A gasp of cold air escaped, and the butterfly fluttered inside.

Charlie hesitated, his body awash with adrenaline. The butterfly's soft glow faded into the darkened cavern, winking good-bye with the flutter of its illuminated wings.

Or was it beckoning him once again?

Charlie waited only a moment before deciding it wanted him to follow. And so he did.

Michael stood dumbfounded on the edge of the clearing.

Charlie had disappeared.

Not only that, but he'd also disappeared into a mystical doorway in the side of a cliff.

And the door had closed behind him.

Dawn crept across the clearing, spreading its warm glow over the island. Michael cast a backward glance at the forest, then sprinted across the field toward the tree, minding the thick roots that lined the earth like veins.

He clutched the still-pulsing wound. When blood had soaked his makeshift bandage a while back, he abandoned it and made a fresh one from his other sleeve. Fortunately, the bleeding had slowed.

Michael reached the side of the tree where its trunk met the cliff's face. He peered up into its darkened branches, then drew his eyes down to the place where Charlie had disappeared.

A feeling of anticipation overtook Michael's body. His heart pounded in his ears. He lifted his bandaged hand, then hesitated, feeling the air pulse around his fingers. For a moment he wondered if the sensation came from the wound, but now the subtle vibration thrummed through his whole body, electrifying every cell with wonder and desire.

Michael touched the rock's cool surface, and the mysterious door yawned open. Without even a second of hesitation, Michael walked inside.

Charlie paused inside the cavern and turned in time to see the rock wall seal. Darkness surrounded him, and the sound of scraping rock rumbled through the cavelike structure. Dread washed over Charlie, rooting his feet to the stone floor. A gust of damp air came from the tunnel where the butterfly had disappeared. Charlie turned to see the faint flicker of its wings drifting deeper into the cavern. Another light glimmered beyond it.

Swallowing his fear, Charlie walked toward the light, grazing a hand on the cold surface of the rock tunnel.

He rounded a corner and saw a lit torch hanging from the wall not ten yards in front of him.

"How did that get here?" Charlie whispered, remembering that Michael had said there were no other people on the island.

The soft glow of the butterfly drifted beyond the torch, leading the way. There seemed to be a room at the end of the corridor. Charlie continued and paused when he reached the light. There was something on the wall.

Handwriting.

Written in a red, chalklike substance were the words *Dream Travelers were here.*

A shiver ran the length of Charlie's spine. This island became stranger by the moment.

He picked up the torch, then hurried down the last few feet of the tunnel and entered a small circular room hewn into the rock. The butterfly waited on the wall near the entrance.

Charlie stepped into the center of the round space. It was no more than ten feet in diameter.

"Where are we?" he said aloud.

As if in response, the butterfly fluttered up from the wall and made a slow lap through the cave, drawing Charlie's attention to every inch of the circular stone room. It paused when it reached the back wall, hovering; then it came to rest.

A sound echoed behind Charlie.

Footsteps.

The butterfly pulsed its wings quickly and fled the wall, flying back toward the room's entrance.

Charlie turned.

The light from the torch illuminated the opening and the person standing inside it—Michael.

"Hey, Chucky," Michael said.

Charlie backed away from him into the strange stone room.

Michael scanned the cavern with his eyes, his mind racing with questions.

Where were they?

How had Charlie known how to find this place?

And more importantly, what was it?

Michael felt as confused as Charlie looked. But he wasn't about to let Charlie know that. Instead, he pulled his knife from his pocket and flicked it open.

The confusion on Charlie's face morphed into fear.

"What are you doing here?" Charlie asked.

Michael could hear the quiver in his voice. He wanted to ask Charlie the same question. Instead, he said, "Oh, I think you know why I'm here." Michael inched closer.

Charlie backed away again, and Michael saw his eyes flick to the left.

"*What is that?*" Michael asked, seeing a glowing object drift through the air. It flew past Michael's head. He backed away as if it would sting him, then swatted at it when it came close again. Finally it landed on the wall near them.

Michael took a step closer. He felt his eyes widen, not wanting to believe what he was seeing. "Is that a butterfly?"

Charlie moved toward it. "Yeah. Looks like I'm not crazy after all. I followed it here."

Michael glanced at Charlie, then back at the glowing creature. "This thing led you here?"

Charlie nodded. Despite the fear that radiated from Charlie, Michael could see the enchantment in the boy's eyes when he looked at the butterfly. And the slightly smug look on his face at having been right. It infuriated Michael.

His eyes flicked to the butterfly again. Michael hated to admit it, but the creature intrigued him too. But not enough to let his guard down—not with Charlie.

Michael smirked, raised his uninjured hand, then smashed the butterfly against the wall.

Charlie flinched. His face fell.

Michael glanced down at his left hand. A shimmery

residue clung to his fingers. He wiped it onto the front of his shorts.

"Look, Michael," Charlie began. "I'm sorry I pushed you. Really, it was an accident."

"Was it now?" Michael cocked his head to the side. "Seemed like you were pretty mad at me." He stepped closer.

"I *was* mad," Charlie said, stepping backward. "But I never wanted to kill you. You know that. Right, Michael? You know I didn't want to kill you?"

"Yes, Charlie," Michael said. "I *do* know that. I don't think you have it in you to kill someone." Michael lowered his voice. He held up his hand for Charlie to see the faint smears of glowing ooze on his fingers. "But I do." He held Charlie's stare. "You and I both know you weren't trying to kill me. But nobody else will ever know that. Your side of the story will die right here in this weird little cave." Michael smiled. "With you."

Charlie took another step away from him. The torch fell from his hand. Sparks flew as it clattered against the ground.

"There's nowhere else to go, Charlie. No one will even find your body. Unless a butterfly leads them here." Michael felt a smile tug at his lips. "But the butterfly is dead too."

Michael took another step.

Charlie's foot touched the wall, and Michael saw him reach backward as if to brace himself.

Then he vanished.

Michael froze, eyes fixed on the rock wall where Charlie had just stood.

He stepped closer. A warm vibration hummed in the wall.

Michael lifted his left hand, hesitated, then placed his palm against its surface.

Then he fell through the wall and into darkness.

CHAPTER SIX

THE ROCK WALL GAVE WAY behind Charlie. He fell to the ground and rolled onto his back. A darkness thicker than anything he'd ever experienced wrapped itself around his body in an oppressive weight. Charlie blinked to ensure his eyes were open.

They were.

He groped in the dark, searching for the wall. It was gone, replaced by the texture of rough wooden floorboards and walls made of the same material.

Charlie hesitated, then stood, feeling through the darkness with his hands. He brushed against something like a wooden rack. Cool glass greeted his fingertips as he carefully felt along the shelves to investigate their contents. Jars, he guessed, dozens of them, and a large coarse object, like a canvas sack, which sat beside them. Charlie took a small step backward and tripped, knocking over several objects as he stumbled.

A loud clatter filled what Charlie could now tell was a small space, but thankfully nothing shattered. He moved his hands along the floor for the object that had tripped him. His fingers grazed something long and wooden. When he picked it up, he touched the bristles on the other end. A broom?

Am I in a closet?

Charlie turned in the darkness with cautious arms outstretched. A thin strip of amber light glowed along the floor on one wall. With his eyes now adjusted, he could tell it flickered like firelight.

Like the torch he'd dropped.

He searched the door for a handle. When he found it, he hesitated. The cool metal of the knob sent a chill up his arm. Charlie hoped Michael was not still on the other side waiting to greet him with his knife.

He edged the door open and dared a glance outside, prepared to see the torchlit cavern. Instead, a warm candlelit kitchen welcomed him. Charlie pushed the door open all the way and stepped into the strange space.

The room was rustic, like something out of a story-book. Wooden shelves lined the walls, filled with dried spices and salts. A large butcher-block counter sat in the center of the room. Candlelight flickered against a flat piece of metal resting on its surface. Charlie glanced both ways before approaching. He ran his fingers over the smooth wood. Dark reddish-brown blotches stained the grain.

It was blood.

And the metal object he'd seen from across the room was a cleaver.

Charlie backed away.

Where am I?

The clomp of horses' hooves sounded in the distance. Charlie spun to see a closed door in another wall. Large hunks of curing meat dangled from the ceiling on either side. A bloodied apron hung from a hook on the door.

The sound of the horses was louder now, and a few seconds later, he heard them pass. He approached the door, assuming it led outside. The sound of laughter and voices reached him from beyond. He paused a moment with his ear to the wooden door. There were many voices, perhaps even a crowd.

Feeling more confused than before, Charlie pulled open the door and stepped out onto a bustling cobblestone street.

To the left, a horse-drawn cart receded down a torchlit corridor. It appeared to be the middle of the night, which was odd, since the first light of dawn had been creeping across the field when Charlie entered the strange cliffside door behind that gnarled tree.

On the island …

Charlie took in his surroundings. This certainly didn't look like any part of the island he had ever seen.

He turned to close the door behind him and noticed a sign over the lintel that read *Butcher*.

Yes, he was sure no one had said anything about a butcher's shop on the island.

People hurried about their business, none of them paying Charlie any attention. They wore homespun clothes of brown, black, and gray fabrics: long skirts and dresses for the women, tunics and slacks for the men. They looked like characters from a medieval-period movie.

Charlie took a cautious step into the bustling street. A man on a horse galloped past, forcing him to dart back. After catching his breath, Charlie scanned the storefronts across from the butcher's shop. Each one was candlelit. The billowy fabrics of ladies' gowns hung in one display window, and beside it, a grocer's display of fruits and vegetables lined the next storefront. A man with greasy hair stacked canvas sacks beside a bushel of apples. The word *flour* marked the dingy canvas.

People darted in and out of the torchlit storefronts purchasing groceries, clothing, and other goods. Charlie couldn't understand how the street was so busy at night.

More importantly, he couldn't understand what street this was.

Moments ago, he'd been in an eerie cave on a deserted island. Now he stood in the center of what looked to be a renaissance market.

Thinking of the butterfly that led him here, Charlie landed on the one logical conclusion he could make.

"This is a dream," he said to himself.

"What's a dream?"

Charlie jumped and turned to see a small elderly woman standing beside him. She held a waxed-paper-wrapped parcel in her knobby fingers. Deep creases lined her face, and her mouth sank in like a soft bruise on a piece of fruit. She flashed Charlie a toothless grin.

The weathered woman was at least an inch shorter than Charlie, her back rounded and shoulders curled. She wore a cloak with a hood that draped her wiry gray hair.

She repeated her question. "What's a dream?"

Charlie didn't answer and instead asked, "Who are you?"

"Who am I? The better question is *who are you*?" She narrowed milky gray eyes at him. Her pupils were nearly as large as her irises, and a foggy film covered the lenses.

Charlie scanned the street once more, overwhelmed by confusion.

"My name's Charlie," he said, turning back to her.

"Charlie," she repeated. "You aren't from around here, are you, Charlie?" Her hazy eyes scanned him from head to toe. In his dirty white T-shirt, shorts, and tennis shoes, Charlie didn't exactly blend in with the crowd.

"Come here and let me have a look at you." She motioned for Charlie to lean down. "I don't bite," she chuckled in a hoarse voice.

Charlie hesitated, then obliged.

"Your eyes," the woman said in an awe-filled whisper. "So unusual. I've heard tales of a people with eyes like yours, but legend says they've long since been extinct."

Charlie started to ask her for clarification, but she continued.

"So where are you from then?" she asked.

Charlie debated how he should answer: from Montana? An island? Or a weird cave with magical doors? Eventually he said, "I'm from Saint Francis's Boys and Girls Home in Montana."

"Oh!" she said excitedly. "Francis? I heard he came to visit once. A long time ago. But, of course, many people say that's just a legend as well." She didn't offer him the chance to speak. "Where's Montana?" she asked.

Charlie furrowed his brow.

Yeah, this definitely had to be a dream.

"In the United States," Charlie said.

The right side of her sunken mouth pinched together. Her milky eyes peered up as if searching the deep recesses of her memory. "Never heard of it," she said with a shrug.

Charlie started to say something, then stopped. He pressed his lips together.

"Well," the elderly woman continued, "welcome to Lumina then, capital city of Eydon."

"Eydon?" Charlie felt as if he'd traveled to another planet. "And Lumina?"

The woman nodded. "Best of the twelve cities if you ask me. And I would know. I used to travel quite a bit as a young woman."

This dream was becoming stranger by the moment.

Charlie gestured to the street. "Why is the market so busy in the middle of the night?"

"Middle of the night?" The woman bubbled with laughter. "Boy, it's the middle of the day! My, my, you certainly aren't from around here." Her laughter drifted off. "Oh!" Her eyes went wide, and she gestured for Charlie to step closer. She grabbed his forearm and pulled him toward the building. "Look!" She pointed and spoke in a raspy whisper.

Charlie followed her finger. Two hard-faced men

approached from the left, heads shaved, muscular bodies draped in matching brown robes. White ropey cords belted their waists and held long daggers swinging in their sheaths. Both men—one dark skinned and one light—had gray eyes that matched the old woman's. She dug her arthritic fingers into Charlie's arm.

"That's the Sovereign Guard," she hissed. She pushed Charlie away from them. "I'd run if I were you."

"Run?"

"Yes," she said. "Go! Quickly!"

Charlie didn't dare ask another question. The urgency in the woman's voice was enough to spur him down the street. His tennis shoes slapped the cobblestone with a rhythmic thump, thump, thump.

Behind him he heard a male voice shout. "Look! There!"

Charlie quickened his pace.

"You there! Boy! Halt!"

Ahead, a corridor split the row of shops. Charlie raced toward the alley and dashed down the darkened street. Another row of vendors stretched before him, and now, people were paying attention to the brown boy with golden eyes.

Footfalls sounded behind him.

"This way!" someone shouted. "He went this way!"

The pounding of footsteps grew louder, closer.

Charlie darted around a bread cart, knocking

over several loaves as he passed. He pushed his legs to sprint faster and hurried around a corner into another torchlit alley.

This one was a dead end.

"Boy! Halt!"

Charlie turned. The two men called the Sovereign Guard filled the entrance to the alley with their impressive girth. Their boots clomped as they approached. Charlie stepped back, his shoe landing in a puddle. Their milky gray eyes pierced him with a menacing gaze.

"Up here!" a voice from above shouted.

Charlie looked up to see a red-haired, freckle-faced girl peering over the side of the building's rooftop. She beckoned him with her hand.

"This way! Up the ladder." She pointed to a ladder at the back of the alley, five feet from where he stood.

Charlie didn't stop to think. He just reacted and obeyed the stranger, who seemed to be helping him.

He darted for the ladder and scaled its damp rungs. Mere feet from the top, his right foot slipped. He barely caught himself. The guards were below him now, one already on the first rung.

"C'mon!" the girl shouted to Charlie as he swung a leg over the top of the flat-roofed building. When he stood, the view behind her made Charlie stop.

From here, he could see the darkened landscape

littered with amber torchlight. The moon hung suspended like a silver coin against a black velvet blanket. More stars than Charlie had ever seen glittered against the night. And in the near distance, he could see what looked like the city center, where a towering firelit spire protruded from a massive stone building. A courtyard surrounded it.

"We don't have time to gawk." The girl's hand wrapped around his wrist. "Let's go," she said. She yanked hard on his arm and pulled Charlie across the roof. He heard the guard behind them but didn't look back.

The girl led him to the edge of the building and pointed to the rooftop of the shop next door. "Jump!" she shouted, then she leapt into the darkness, leaving Charlie alone with a Sovereign Guard close on his heels. The man drew his dagger.

Charlie didn't dare glance over the side. If he did, he'd never jump. Instead, he fixed his eyes on the glowing spire in the distance and plunged over the edge.

He landed on all fours and scrambled to keep his footing on the thatched and steeply angled roof. His eyes searched the darkness for the girl. She stood atop the peak.

"C'mon!" she yelled.

Charlie scaled the slippery surface and scrambled toward the top. When he reached the highest point, he saw the girl slide down the other side and drop to the ground. Charlie followed suit and landed in another alley. His feet hit cobblestone, and he was off again, following the rag-clad stranger.

"There they are!" a male voice shouted.

Charlie cast a glance over his shoulder to see the guards standing on the roof and pointing down at the two kids.

"Hurry!" the girl said.

Charlie's legs felt like they would fail him. The burn in his lungs was unbearable. And despite the ever-present torches, the darkness was difficult to navigate. But the redheaded girl had no trouble.

With every labored breath he drew, Charlie realized this felt less and less like a dream. The adrenaline that coursed through his veins felt incredibly real. As did the sweat that dripped down his back.

Fear washed over him, but Charlie didn't have time to process or try to make sense of his surroundings. He certainly didn't have time to stop and ask his rescuer any questions.

Only one thought consumed his mind now: *don't stop running.*

"This way," the girl said.

The road split, and Charlie followed her to the right. Ahead of them, a pair of horses pulled a cart filled with straw down the street.

The girl glanced back at Charlie. "You got anything left?"

"Huh?"

"Run!" she said. "As fast as you can!" And then she was off, sprinting toward the cart.

Charlie couldn't understand how she was able to move so fast when they'd already run so far, but he shoved the thought into the back of his mind.

The girl leapt into the back of the straw cart and was covering herself with hay.

Charlie pushed his body to its limit. Legs sprinted. Arms pumped at his sides. Breath burned in the back of his throat. And then he was almost there. He flung his body at the cart but nearly missed it. The girl thrust out a hand from the straw and pulled hard on his arm. Her grip burned the flesh on Charlie's wrist. But he was in, covering himself with straw as she had done.

"Shhh!" he heard her say from somewhere in the stack.

Charlie pressed his lips together and sucked air through his nose. His breathing sounded impossibly loud in the confined space.

Muffled by the straw and clomp of hooves, Charlie heard a male voice say, "Where'd they go?"

"You said they went this way," the other man responded.

"I thought they did. Must've gone over here."

Their voices faded, but Charlie didn't dare move until he felt the girl sit up beside him.

"They're gone," she said.

Charlie sat up.

"Stay low," she cautioned.

Charlie ducked his head. He could feel the straw sticking to his curls. He panted. "Who are you?"

"Name's Brynn." She thrust a freckled hand toward him.

Charlie shook it, noticing her milky gray eyes and enormous pupils.

"What's going on?" he asked. "Where am I? And why are those guys chasing me?"

Brynn shook her head. "No time for questions. Where's your brother? We need to find him too. I'm supposed to take you both to the Sage."

"Brother?"

"Yeah, your brother," Brynn said.

A lightheaded feeling washed over Charlie. "I don't understand."

An irritated expression crossed her face. "What's your name?" she asked.

Charlie hesitated. Ice formed in his veins. "My name's Charlie."

She nodded. "Okay so *you're* Charlie." Her hazy eyes scanned his face. "Then where's your brother, Michael?"

Chapter Seven

MICHAEL BOLTED UPRIGHT, gasping and soaking wet. Mere seconds ago he'd stood in a strange torchlit cavern and touched a rock wall after seeing Charlie disappear through it. Michael's hand had passed through the stone as if it were a hologram, then he fell forward, dropping several feet into darkness and into … Where was he? Michael wiped water from his eyes and took in his surroundings.

He was in a fountain.

An oppressive darkness hovered around him, and the sound of crickets reached his ears. Michael paused, listening to their sound.

"Weird," he whispered, remembering that Kurtis had insisted there were no insects on the island. Then again, just minutes ago, he'd smashed a glowing butterfly against a cave wall. Michael shook his head, flinging water droplets from his curly hair.

His eyes began to adjust to the darkness, revealing what looked to be an elaborate courtyard. Intricately pruned evergreens formed a row of geometric shapes in front of him and lined a ten-foot-high stone wall. Torchlight illuminated the grounds and cast strange shadows against the lawn where cobblestone pavers intermingled with lush grass. The soft gurgle of the fountain melded with the rhythmic chirp of crickets.

Michael turned. Two other similar fountains were visible in the darkness. A paved path wove around the circular water features and led to a building no more than a hundred yards in the distance. Michael swept his eyes up the stone façade of the structure to the top of the spire. Torches illuminated the steeple. Michael squinted in the darkness, expecting to see a bell framed by the four arched openings, but there was none. Instead, ambient firelight glittered off a reflective surface that lined the inside of the tower.

Michael stood to get a better view of his surroundings. He took a step forward, slipped, then landed with a loud splash. A thin layer of algae coated the tiled bottom of the fountain. Michael balled his hands into fists and smacked them against the surface of the water. A wave of anger washed over him and mingled with his confusion.

Where was he?

And where was Charlie?

Grabbing hold of the edge of the fountain, Michael pulled himself to his feet and swung his leg over the side. Water poured from his soaked clothes and puddled on the cobblestone pavers. His feet squished in his shoes.

"You, there! Halt!"

Michael spun.

Four men with shaved heads, dressed in brown robes, stood on the other side of the large fountain. Each one held a drawn dagger.

"You don't have authorization to be here!" one of the men barked.

Michael didn't know where *here* was, but the strange men with drawn daggers made his heart race. He took a step back.

"This is a mistake," Michael said, his eyes now fully adjusted to the darkness.

The intimidating monklike men divided into pairs; one set flanked the right side of the fountain while the other two came around the left side.

Michael stepped back again.

"State your name, boy," one of the men said.

Michael held up his hands in surrender but continued to inch his way backward toward an opening he'd seen in the courtyard wall. "I'm leaving," Michael said.

"This is all a big misunderstanding. I don't know how I got here."

The men shared a suspicious glance but said nothing. They advanced on him quickly.

Michael spun and ran toward the arched opening. He darted through the passageway but slammed into something solid. He backed away to see a man who was every bit of six and half feet tall. He, too, bore a shaved head and brown robe. But his dagger remained sheathed and swung from a rope belt tied around his waist. Firelight flickered in the man's eyes, illuminating a milky-white film that covered gray irises and unusually large pupils. He narrowed his gaze.

Michael tried to dart to the right, but the man blocked him.

"I was just leaving," Michael insisted.

A viselike grip locked around Michael's wrist, and the man dragged him toward the fountain and the other four creepy monks. Michael struggled against the man's hold, but only managed to twist his arm into an even more uncomfortable position.

"I heard splashing," Michael's captor said to his comrades. He pushed Michael forward but didn't release his wrist.

"So did we," one of the other monks said. "Looks like he's another one of those street urchins. Just throw him in the dungeon and—" He paused, scanning Michael up and down. "What's he wearing?"

Michael glanced down at his dirty green Hawaiian print shirt. The sleeves were missing, and the fabric from one protected his injured palm. Blood and soil stained his khaki shorts.

"I don't think he's a street urchin," the man who held Michael's wrist said. He tightened his grip, yanked on Michael's arm, and pulled him into a ring of light cast by the nearest torch. He tipped Michael's chin upward. "Look at his eyes."

The others stepped closer, and in the light of the torch, Michael could see that their eyes matched the cloudy gray of the man who held him.

The five men exchanged glances. Their silence spoke volumes. Michael really shouldn't be here.

"The Sovereign will want to see him right away," one of them said.

"I'll take him," Michael's captor said.

The four parted and made way for their leader to drag Michael across the lawn toward the castlelike structure.

"Where am I?" Michael demanded. "Who are you? And where are you taking me?" He looked up into the man's face. The monk's chiseled jaw flexed with irritation.

When he said nothing, Michael repeated, "Where am I?"

"You should mind your tongue, boy," the man said. "You're about to enter the House of Lumina. You don't speak unless you're spoken to."

Michael's mind whirled as the man pulled him up the stone slab steps toward the entrance. A massive pair of wooden paneled doors swung inward as they approached. Two other monks waited inside, holding the doors open. They said nothing as Michael and his captor entered.

The squeak of Michael's wet tennis shoes against the marble floor echoed off the vaulted ceiling. Torches lined the smooth stone walls of the foyer. Their light flickered over the man's hardened face as he pulled Michael down a long corridor. Another pair of opulent wooden doors beckoned them. A sense of dread overwhelmed Michael.

"Who's the Sovereign?" Michael dared to ask. His voice sounded too loud in the silent hallways of the House of Lumina.

The imposing man shot him a threatening stare, then said, "Who are you and where are you from that you don't know the Sovereign of Lumina—the highest authority in all of Eydon?" He prodded Michael with his eyes. "Go on then. Speak, since you're so fond of doing so. Where are you from, boy?"

"I—uh …" Michael stammered. "I'm from Montana."

The man furrowed his brow and narrowed his cloudy eyes. "Montana? Is that one of the precincts in Valo? How'd you get all the way here?"

Michael hesitated, unsure how to answer. "Uh … I don't know."

Lumina the man had said. Michael searched his brain for any clue that might help him understand what was happening, but he came up empty.

The man huffed and yanked Michael forward. "You will answer to the Sovereign," he said.

Michael's captor didn't speak another word as he led him down the remainder of the corridor and through the wooden doors. Michael froze when his feet crossed the threshold.

The doors, held open by two brown-robed men, led into a vast chamber, where a black marble floor extended the length of a football field and ended in an ornate dais. Firelight glinted off the floor's polished surface, and slate-gray pillars flanked the aisle. A torch hung from each of the columns and warmed the darkened space. Candlestands made of an onyx-colored metal lined both sides of the dais. A grand throne that seemed to be carved from black wood sat in the center of the raised platform. The organic and gnarled shape of the royal chair reminded Michael of the tree that had led him into this dreamlike world. The light from the nearby candles illuminated every twist and curve of the strange throne—and the man seated upon it.

"Cyrus!" The voice of the man on the throne bellowed through the chamber and echoed around them. "Please tell me what's so important that you must disturb my afternoon dealings."

"Afternoon?" Michael said under his breath.

The man beside him—Cyrus apparently—silenced Michael with a stare. Without taking his eyes from Michael, he spoke in a pompous voice that carried down the chamber aisle and echoed off the vaulted ceiling. "Your Royal Sovereign, I do apologize for the interruption, but we had an intruder in the courtyards."

The Sovereign looked up from the large ledger book on his lap and cast a dismissive glance in Michael's direction. "If it's another one of those street urchins, then throw him in the dungeons with the others." He turned his attention back to the book. "Honestly, Cyrus, if you were any other guard, I'd have you locked up as well."

Cyrus hesitated before saying, "Sir, I believe you'll want to have a word with this particular intruder."

The Sovereign looked up from the book once more. From this distance, Michael couldn't make out his features, but he didn't like the way the man was scrutinizing him. The Sovereign slammed the book closed, then shouted, "Chancellor!"

A man in a black robe entered from a door in the wall behind the throne. His hooded cloak hid his face from the candlelight. He took the ledger book from the Sovereign's hands and stepped back from the throne but lingered near his master.

The Sovereign crossed one leg over the other, then waved Cyrus and Michael down the center aisle. Water dripped from Michael's clothes and dotted the floor. His wet shoes seemed to squeak even louder than when he was in the hallway, but the Sovereign's cold expression never changed.

"My deepest apologies for the interruption, my lord," Cyrus said. "But considering the boy's appearance, I thought it necessary to bring him to you right away." Cyrus stared down at Michael.

Water puddled around Michael's feet.

"You're wet," the Sovereign said, his voice devoid of emotion.

"He was in the fountain, my lord."

"Let the boy speak for himself, Cyrus." The Sovereign hardened his stare. He, too, bore the same gray eyes with large pupils. A cloudy film covered their surface.

"Why were you in my fountain?" the Sovereign asked. He folded his hands in his lap.

Michael cleared his throat. "I fell in, sir."

"Fell in?"

There was something unsettlingly familiar about the Sovereign. A close-cut blond beard covered his structured cheeks. His hair, also blond, reached his shoulders and curled slightly on the ends. An ornate crown made of the same onyx-colored metal as the candlestands graced his head. A thick black robe hung about his shoulders and draped over the sides of his throne.

"Yes, sir. I fell in."

Irritation flickered on the Sovereign's face. "How?"

Michael drew a deep breath, trying to decide which part of his crazy story he should share: The plane crash? The mysterious doorway that opened into the cliffside behind a nightmarish tree? Or the part about how he seemed to have miraculously transported to another world?

"I'm not sure," Michael finally said.

The Sovereign narrowed his eyes, then beckoned Michael to step closer. "Where are you from, boy?"

"He said he's from Montana, sir," Cyrus answered. "A precinct in Valo, I believe."

"There's no precinct in all of Eydon called Montana," the Sovereign said. Turning to Michael he asked, "What's your name?"

"Michael, sir."

The Sovereign started to speak again, then paused. He pressed his thin lips together and uncrossed his legs. "Tell me, Michael of Montana, how is it you have such unusual eyes."

Michael wanted to turn the question back on the Sovereign. Instead he said, "Where I come from, everyone has eyes like mine. Well, not like mine exactly. But everyone has colored eyes: brown, blue, green, like me. To be honest, sir, it's *your* eyes that seem unusual."

The sound of a dagger being unsheathed filled the chamber. Michael turned to see Cyrus with his weapon drawn.

The Sovereign held up a hand. "Put it away, Cyrus. My honor is not so easily offended. And especially not by a boy with green eyes." The Sovereign turned to the Chancellor. They exchanged glances. To Michael he said, "What happened to your hand? Did one of my men do this to you?"

Michael glanced down at the hand wrapped with his shirt sleeve. He held it up for the Sovereign to see. "No. It was an accident. I cut myself with—"

"*What is that?*" The Sovereign leaned forward in his chair; his cloudy eyes narrowed.

"A bandage, well, a part of my shirt that I made into a bandage—"

"No, not that. *That.*" The Sovereign stood, descended

the raised platform, and crossed the short distance between them. He grabbed Michael's wrist and dug his fingers into his flesh.

"Ow!" Michael tried to yank his arm away, but the Sovereign was unfazed.

He pointed to the star-shaped birthmark on the inside of Michael's right forearm. "Where did you get this?" Ice filled the Sovereign's voice.

This time, Michael managed to pull his arm away. "From my parents," he sneered. "It's a birthmark. What? Don't you have birthmarks here in your weird city?"

"Watch your tongue," the Sovereign warned. "I'm the Sovereign. I ask the questions. Now, who are your parents? Tell me."

Michael rubbed the welt forming on his wrist. "I don't know. I'm an orphan, okay?" Under his breath, he said, "I thought your honor wasn't so easily offended."

The Sovereign exchanged another glance with his Chancellor. For the first time, the man removed his hood. Milky gray eyes were the first thing Michael noticed when the Chancellor stepped down from the dais and came to stand beside his master.

The Chancellor leaned forward to examine Michael's eyes, paused, then leaned back. He turned from Michael to exchange another silent glance with the Sovereign.

Michael swallowed and shifted from foot to foot.

"Tell me again how you arrived here," the Sovereign said.

Michael sighed. "You wouldn't believe me if I told you."

"Try me."

Michael shook his head. If they weren't going to lock him up for trespassing, they'd certainly put him away once they realized he was crazy.

"Okay, so I was in a plane crash," Michael began. "We landed on an island, and I found this tree." Michael pointed to the throne seat. "The wood of its trunk kind of looked like that, actually." The Sovereign said nothing, so Michael continued. "Anyway, there was a rocky cliff behind the tree, and a door that opened into it." He skipped the part about his plans to kill Charlie. "Inside there was a round room. I touched the back wall and *poof.* I landed in your fountain. There. You happy?"

The Sovereign straightened his shoulders and took a step back. "This isn't possible," he muttered.

"I said you wouldn't believe me."

"No. Not that." The Sovereign turned and finally spoke to the Chancellor. "It's not possible, is it? He's not even the right age."

Confused, Michael asked, "What are you talking about?"

"True, my lord," the Chancellor said. "But there is the time difference."

The Sovereign rubbed a hand over his short blond beard, then slowly returned to his throne. "But how?"

Michael heard Cyrus shift behind him.

After several agonizingly silent seconds, the Sovereign lowered himself to the seat and answered his own question. "This is clearly the work of the Sage," he said.

"And Josephine, my lord," the Chancellor added. "You suspected she sent the boys away, and now the Sage has brought them back through the portal."

The Sovereign stroked his beard. His lips twitched to the side. "And there's only one reason the Sage would bring them back." He pierced Michael with a hazy stare. "To overthrow my kingdom."

Silence lingered in the Sovereign's chambers.

Michael's mind whirled with questions.

Finally, the Sovereign pointed at Michael and said, "But how can we be certain this boy is my son?"

"Your son?" Michael took a step forward, but Cyrus caught his arm and yanked him back.

The Chancellor cleared his throat. "My lord, if I may be so bold—he looks like you."

And as soon as he'd said it, Michael realized why the Sovereign was familiar. The cut of his jawline, the high cheek bones …

They were the same as Michael's.

Even Michael's hair color could have come from this man. He ran his free hand over his light-brown curls that faded to blond at the ends. Though he'd never known his mother or father, Michael had always known from his own complexion that one of his parents was black and one was white.

Michael's knees went weak. Could this man be his father?

"My lord," the Chancellor said, "it must be him. There's no other explanation. Clearly, this boy is your son."

"I'm dreaming," Michael said. "I have to be dreaming."

"Well, *my son*," the Sovereign said, drawing out his words, "if it *is* a dream, then it's about to become a nightmare."

Michael's legs failed him, but Cyrus held him upright.

"How can I be your son?" Michael asked. His voice wavered. "*Why* do you think I'm your son?" A torrent of emotions swarmed inside of him.

"The mark on your arm," the Sovereign said. "A birthmark is unique, and one of my boys—the lighter of the two—had a star-shaped birthmark exactly like the one you bear."

"What do you mean *one of your boys*?" A light-headed feeling washed over Michael.

The Sovereign snapped his fingers. "Guard!" Another one of the soldierlike monks appeared from the shadows of the chamber. He sidled up next to Michael and Cyrus and took hold of Michael's other arm.

"I had two children with my wife, Josephine," the Sovereign explained. "Twin boys."

"Twins?" The word came out as an exhale from Michael's lips.

"Yes, my wife—traitorous woman that she is—opposed my reign. She ran off with my sons—you and your brother—and sent you both through a portal to another world to keep you from my influence."

Michael couldn't even speak.

"She abandoned you," the Sovereign said with a tilt of his head. "She abandoned both of you. All in an attempt to overthrow my kingdom. No doubt she planned to bring you back one day when I least expected it. Of course, she couldn't do it herself." The Sovereign glanced at the Chancellor. "This whole situation reeks of the Sage. Well, it's too late now. I've foiled the Sage's plan by finding you before he did." The Sovereign steepled his fingers in front of his chest and smiled.

"There's still one problem, my lord," the Chancellor said. "Charles."

Michael blinked. "Charles?"

"Yes," the Sovereign said. "Your twin brother, Charles. He must have come through the portal with you. The Sage would've brought you both. Tell me. Where is your brother?"

Michael's thoughts clicked into place, and the swarm of emotions he felt moments before filtered down to one—hatred.

Charlie.

Of course, it had to be Charlie.

"Where's your brother?" the Sovereign repeated.

"I don't know," Michael admitted through gritted teeth.

"But he came through with you?" the Sovereign asked. "He's here? In Lumina?"

Michael closed his eyes and drew a sharp breath through his nostrils. When he opened his eyes, he said, "He came through the portal. That's all I know."

"Very well, then." The Sovereign stood. "Chancellor, come with me. We have much to discuss."

The Sovereign stood and the two of them turned toward the door in the wall behind the throne.

"What about me?" Michael shouted at their backs.

The Sovereign stopped and turned. "What about you?" he said.

"You said I'm your son." Michael paused. "What will happen to me?"

The Sovereign's emotionless eyes scanned Michael one final time. "You may be born of my blood," he said, "but you are nothing to me." Then looking to Cyrus and the other guard, he said, "Throw him in a cell with the other urchins."

The Sovereign's words echoed through the chamber. They were the last thing Michael heard as the guards dragged him from his father's presence and ushered him through the halls of the House of Lumina to the dungeons.

CHAPTER EIGHT

MORNING LIGHT WARMED Sarah's face. She stirred awake. Beside her, Maxine was still asleep. She shifted away from the girl and sat up.

"Yup. Still on an island." Sarah groaned, rubbed the sleep from her eyes, then brushed the sand from her arms. Despite her sleeping on top of the tarp, sand managed to cling to her body. She couldn't get away from it. It filled her shoes, her socks, even the pockets of her skort, which was now filthy. A small tear marred the hem.

Sarah peered over at the boys' tarp. Empty. She and Maxine were the last to wake. Even Charlie was no longer asleep on the blue plastic sheet. She bit the inside of her lip, regretting the way she'd left things with him. Yes, Charlie had hurt Sarah with his comments. But she knew she'd hurt him too. Perhaps even worse.

She'd never seen Charlie as infuriated as he was

yesterday. Usually, he managed to control his anger, especially toward Michael. But something Michael had said wormed its way into Charlie's brain. Charlie hadn't told Sarah what Michael said that made him snap, only that Michael crossed the line.

It seemed Sarah had too.

She stood, and Maxine stirred awake.

"Where are you going?" the girl asked.

Sarah tucked her soiled white polo shirt into her skort out of habit. "To find Charlie," she said. "I want to make sure he's okay after yesterday. We were pretty hard on him."

"But he pushed Michael," Maxine said.

"I know." Sarah sighed and dusted the sand from her skort. "But Michael pushed him too—emotionally at least. I know what Charlie did seems worse, but we're all under a lot of stress here." Sarah picked up her uniform blazer, which she'd used as a pillow. She tied it around her waist. "We need to show each other some grace. We're all in this together."

Maxine stood beside her. "I don't think Michael's going to forgive Charlie."

Sarah nodded. "I know. That's why *I* need to forgive him."

Maxine gave her a quizzical look.

"Charlie and I had a fight yesterday," she explained.

Maxine was the first and only person she'd told. "But he's my best friend," Sarah said. "Surely, I can forgive my best friend."

"And your enemies," Maxine said. "Like that verse we read in class."

Sarah glanced across the beach and saw several of the children but not Charlie. She turned back to Maxine. "Just like that," she said. "Let's hope he can forgive me too."

Sarah walked down the beach with Maxine in tow. Milo had lit another fire in the firepit he and Raegan had built. Most of the children sat around it, eyes still bleary with sleep and chins glistening with juice from the mangos they were eating.

"Good morning," Sarah said.

Tyler grunted something indiscernible.

"Morning," Becca said.

Joey sat beside her. Though he was two years older than Maxine, he somehow appeared younger. Angst lingered on his freckled face.

Sarah knew all the children were still scared—including her—but a sense of resolve had taken up residence within them. They were stuck here until rescue came. They had to make the most of their situation if they were to survive.

Sarah picked up a mango from the pile and handed

it to Maxine. "Has anyone seen Charlie?" She grabbed one for herself.

Tyler glanced up from his mango and shot her a look. "I'm not his keeper."

Sarah folded her arms over her chest, mango in one hand. "No," she said. "You're not. I'm just curious if you saw him."

"I saw him." Milo poked the fire with a stick, coaxing the flames higher.

Sarah started to peel the fruit with her dirty fingernails.

"Last night." Milo pointed a finger toward the tree line without looking up from the firepit. "He went into the woods."

"What?" Sarah dropped the mango and turned in the direction Milo had pointed. "Did he come back?"

"Nope," Milo said.

Sarah waited for further explanation, heart thrumming in her chest, but Milo gave her none.

Tyler threw the skin of his mango in the flames and wiped his sticky hands on the front of his blue Hawaiian print shirt. "Maybe a polar bear ate Charlie," he jeered.

Sarah shot him a stare. "Not funny."

"Yeah," Milo said. "Like that show *Lost*."

Sarah felt Maxine press up against her.

Kurtis scoffed. "There are no polar bears on this island. Besides, it would be far more likely that a snake or spider killed him."

"Not helping, Kurtis," Sarah said.

Kurtis shrugged. "Well, at least there's no snakes or spiders on this island." He paused then added, "That we know of."

"Could have been Michael." Milo prodded the fire again, and sparks flew up.

Sarah hesitated. "What do you mean, 'Could have been Michael?'" she asked.

"Michael could have killed Charlie."

Sarah froze. "Why do you say that?"

Milo shrugged. "Because Michael followed him into the woods."

She felt lightheaded. "Why didn't you tell us that sooner?"

Milo finally looked up. "You didn't ask."

Sarah could tell from his look of confusion that Milo genuinely couldn't understand why she was so upset.

"So did they come back?" Sarah pressed him, realizing she would have to spell out all her questions if she was going to get any answers from the twelve-year-old boy.

"I don't know. I fell asleep after that."

Sarah rubbed her brow. "Okay, well, this is bad." She dropped her hand and looked at the group. "We need to go look for them."

"Maybe we shouldn't jump to conclusions," Kurtis said.

Tyler caught Sarah's eye.

Kurtis pushed his glasses up his nose. "I mean they could be off—"

"Off what?" Sarah demanded. "Off becoming best friends?" She caught Tyler's stare again. "This is Charlie and Michael we're talking about." She turned back to Kurtis. "I think we can all agree that history points to this being a bad situation. We need to find them."

Tyler stood and brushed off his shorts. "I hate to admit it, but I think Sarah's right. Let's go." He patted Maxine on the head as he stepped away from the group. "You coming, Squirt?" he asked her.

"No." Becca stood up. "She's not. She's staying here with me and Joey on the beach."

"No," Sarah said. "We all need to go. We need to find Charlie and Michael, and we need to find them now."

Becca was insistent. "Someone needs to stay on the beach in case a rescue plane comes."

"Becca," Sarah began, "they will see our camp and know we're here. We need everyone's help so we can find them as quickly as possible." She paused. "I'm worried about them. We need to leave now."

Becca held Sarah's gaze for a moment, then huffed. "Fine."

"Good." Sarah grabbed Maxine's hand and motioned for the others to join them. "C'mon," she said. "Let's find them."

Under her breath she said, "And hope we're not too late."

✦✦✦

"It's been an hour," Sarah heard Kurtis say. "And we've found nothing. It shouldn't be that hard to find them on an island this small."

"Just keep looking," Sarah said.

The group had spread out per Sarah's suggestion, but everyone remained within shouting distance of one another.

"Charlie!" Sarah called. "Michael!"

Her voice was hoarse from yelling. As each minute passed without so much as a sign of either boy, her fears heightened. Already her mind raced with horrible possibilities. The last time she'd seen the boys together, Charlie and Michael had been at each other's throats. A pit formed in her stomach.

"Hey, I found something," Raegan shouted.

Sarah's head snapped in Raegan's direction. She saw the girl at a distance, sweat glistening on her forehead as she stooped. Sarah rushed toward her, and the others soon followed.

"What is it?" Sarah asked before she was close enough to see.

Milo approached from the other side of Raegan. His eyes widened when he reached her.

The older girl held up her find.

Sarah halted.

Tyler appeared beside her and stiffened when he saw what Raegan held.

A bloodied cloth—specifically, a green Hawaiian print cloth.

Sarah's stomach plummeted.

"Is that blood?" Maxine asked.

"That's Michael's shirt," Joey said, his voice dripping with fear.

"Michael's?" Maxine's voice was quiet. "What does that mean?"

Milo took a step closer to Sarah and Raegan, eyes fixed on the cloth. He whispered, as if to himself. "It means Charlie killed Michael."

In the silent forest, everyone heard him.

Sarah sensed Tyler turn and stare at her. His eyes bored into the side of her face, but she didn't look at him. Instead, she said, "That's ridiculous, Milo." Sarah took the cloth from Raegan's hand. "And a wild assumption. The only thing we know is that Michael"— she caught herself—"one of them is hurt. All the more reason to find them." She dropped the bloodied cloth.

The looks on the others' faces said they didn't believe Sarah. But she needed them to believe her a little longer, at least until they discovered the truth. Sarah hoped it wasn't as terrible as her imagination could conjure.

"We need to move quickly." She took off ahead of the others in search of Charlie and Michael.

CHAPTER NINE

CHARLIE'S LEGS THROBBED with exhaustion from his sprint with Brynn through the streets of Lumina. His back ached from the cramped ride in the straw cart. It felt like hours before they finally stopped at a small farm outside the city. Just when Charlie believed their travels were over, Brynn ushered him off the cart and into a dense forest behind a barn. A horse waited for them there, tied to a towering sycamore tree.

"We'll follow the creek from here," Brynn said, pointing to the freshwater spring that wound through the woods.

Charlie's eyes followed her finger as she traced the stream all the way up the steep hillside.

"That's where we're going," she said, pointing to its peak. "It's at least an hour's ride."

Brynn didn't say much during their travels, insisting the Sage—whoever he was—would want to explain everything to Charlie. She certainly didn't touch the subject of Charlie's so-called brother, especially after Charlie had insisted he had no brother—and if he did, it certainly wouldn't be anyone named Michael.

The only thing Brynn would talk about was the darkness.

When they began their ride up the winding hillside, it was late afternoon—or so Brynn had said. But the sky hadn't changed. It was still as dark as when the old woman in the streets of Lumina had insisted it was the middle of the day.

"It's always dark here," Brynn said. "You'll get used to it."

"Why's it always dark?" Charlie asked, still wondering if this was just a strange fever dream he was having back on the island.

Brynn shook her head. "I've already said too much."

She didn't speak the rest of their trip. She broke her silence only when they arrived at a quaint stone cottage tucked against the peak of the rocky hillside.

"We're here," she said. "And just in time for dinner."

Charlie stood beside Brynn on the porch. Only one small torch hung in the stand beside the door, but he saw a warm glow behind the drawn curtains in the windows. From the base of the mountain, no one would notice the tiny bungalow behind the towering pines. Charlie smelled the aromatic fragrance of a flower that climbed the porch trellis. Moonlight glimmered off the snow-white petals and illuminated the flowers' crimson-red centers. Moths swarmed the fragrant blossoms.

"Lumina Lilies," Brynn said. "They've always been my favorite."

She rapped her knuckles against the wooden door. Charlie stared at an old rocking chair on the porch while he waited for someone to answer. A moment later, the door creaked open.

A man stood in the doorway, backlit by warm firelight. He wore a rust-colored tunic with a matching robe and pants. A soft-brown leather cord belted his waist. His short, well-kept hair was graying and matched the color of the dense beard that covered his chin. Brightly colored beads held blue feathers in place in his facial hair. Though his face was lined and scarred, suggesting he'd seen much hardship in his lifetime, his eyes were full of kindness.

"Charlie," he said, his voice warm. "My, it's been ages since I last saw you. Please come in."

He held the door open and stepped aside for the two of them to enter.

Charlie heard Brynn pause behind him. "Michael wasn't with him," she whispered.

"I know," the man said in a low voice. "I've already received word. He's in the House of Lumina."

Charlie turned in time to see Brynn's wide eyes and look of horror. She quickly composed herself once she realized Charlie was watching.

"This way," the man said and led them into a large open room.

A stone fireplace centered on the back wall held a large cast-iron pot just above the flames. To the right, a small rustic kitchen featured a simple washbasin and a wooden cart covered with carrots, zucchinis, and jars of spices. To the left, a small hallway led toward what Charlie assumed to be the bedroom area. And a long wooden table occupied the center of the room. Bundles of dried herbs hung from the ceiling rafters above it.

The scent of stew filled the house, and Charlie's stomach growled.

"Please have a seat," the man said.

A loud screech punctuated his sentence. Charlie snapped his attention to the rafters, where a bright-blue parrot stared down at him. It squawked again.

"Don't mind Winny," the man said. "He's just upset you get to have dinner before him."

The bird swooped from the rafters and landed on the back of one of the chairs. It held Charlie's stare with its big eyes, then blinked. Charlie gave it a wide berth as Brynn led him to the table. He sat in the seat farthest from the bird and watched the man retrieve three wooden bowls from a shelf in the kitchen. When he pulled them down, something white zipped across the shelf, then tumbled to the floor. A moment later, a white ferret leapt onto the dining table.

The man shooed the creature with his hand, then took a seat across from Charlie and Brynn and placed a steaming bowl of stew in front of each of them. Charlie's mouth watered. The man gestured to a thick loaf of crusty bread and a dish of salted butter in the center of the table. It took every ounce of restraint Charlie had not to immediately devour the meal.

"You children must be hungry." The man produced wooden spoons and offered them to Charlie and Brynn. "Enjoy," he said.

Brynn plunged her spoon into the stew. She bent over the bowl and shoveled it into her mouth as if she hadn't eaten in days.

Charlie realized he wasn't much better off. After being on the island for two days with little more than mangos and bananas to eat, he appreciated his first hot meal since being at the orphanage.

The man gave Charlie a knowing smile and motioned for him to eat.

Charlie didn't hesitate again.

After devouring two whole bowls of stew and a thick slice of buttered bread, Charlie leaned back in his seat and rested a hand on his stomach.

The man dabbed a napkin on his lips, then brushed breadcrumbs from his beard. He folded the napkin and placed it in his lap.

Charlie saw another flash of white out of the corner of his eye. The ferret had jumped back onto the table and was slinking toward the unfinished loaf of bread.

The man sighed and picked up the creature. Charlie saw the disappointment on its tiny face.

"Are these your pets?" Charlie asked, watching the blue parrot fly from its current perch to the man's shoulder.

"I'd rather think of them as friends," the man said. "Though this one is a rascal." He held up the ferret. "And not mine, I might add. I'm watching him for a friend." The man leaned back in his chair and stroked the ferret's white fur. "Now that you've had a chance to fill your bellies, I believe it's time for some introductions." He smiled warmly. "Charlie, you and I met many years ago, though I doubt you'd remember it. So I'm guessing it's safe to say it's a pleasure to meet you, Charlie. I am the Sage."

Charlie glanced at Brynn, then back at the bearded man. The Sage's kind blue eyes matched the color of the feathers in his beard. For the first time, it occurred to Charlie that this man's eyes were different from the others he'd seen in Lumina. "Nice to meet you," Charlie said.

"Now, I'm sure you have questions—"

"*Many* questions," Charlie said.

"Yes." The Sage chuckled. "*Many* questions. And I will do my best to answer them for you. But first, allow me a moment to get you up to speed. Does that sound okay?"

Charlie nodded.

"All right then." The Sage leaned forward and broke off a piece of bread. He split it in two, giving one piece to the bird and the other to the ferret. "So you've already met Brynn," the Sage said. "And if she's the girl I think she is, then I'm guessing she's been pretty tight-lipped since you've met."

"She wouldn't tell me anything," Charlie said.

"She's good at following orders." The Sage smiled at Brynn, then turned his attention to Charlie. "I knew you'd be overwhelmed, but I thought it best for you to learn everything from me, seeing as I am the one who brought you here to Lumina."

Charlie leaned forward in his chair.

"Brynn is an orphan here in the city and a very good friend of mine. Several other children like her help me out from time to time. I sent her and the others to search for you. You came through the portal on the island, yes?"

Charlie nodded.

The Sage stroked his feathery beard. "Very good. I knew you'd find it. But what I didn't know was where you'd appear here in Lumina once you crossed over."

"How'd you know I'd find it?"

The gray mustache of the Sage's beard curled upward with his smile. "Because you are *from* here, Charlie. From Lumina. It's the city of your birth. I knew this world would draw you to it one way or another." He paused. "And your twin brother, Michael, too."

Charlie flinched. "I only know one Michael, and he's not my brother. And definitely not my twin."

The Sage's brow furrowed. His head tilted slightly. The parrot mimicked his expression. "Michael? From Saint Francis's Boys and Girls Home?" the Sage asked.

Charlie felt the color drain from his face.

"Why, of course he's your brother. I've had eyes on the two of you in the other world since I sent you through the portal together twelve years ago. Well, twelve years ago in your world. Here, it's been twenty-six years. Time works differently here," he explained. "There's not a direct correlation, but it passes much faster here than there."

The parrot screeched. "Twenty-six years," it repeated in a squawky voice. It shifted from foot to foot then bobbed its head up and down. "One, two, three—"

"Shhh …" the Sage said to the bird. "That's very good, but not now." To Charlie, he said, "Winny's working on his counting." He reached up and stroked the parrot's belly. "And you're doing very well," he said to the bird.

"Twenty-six years?" Charlie asked, confusion tinting his voice.

The Sage waved the words away. "It's a small detail. You needn't worry yourself with that." He continued. "Anyway, you and Michael were only a year old when I sent you through the portal to the other world. It was a risk to separate you then, but it would've been an even bigger risk to keep you two together. However"—the Sage arched his eyebrows—"I needed the two of you together once I decided to bring you back to Lumina. It's why I had you transferred from your last foster home to the ranch in Montana. But it sounds like you and Michael didn't exactly bond, am I right?"

"Right," Charlie said in a near whisper. He was too overwhelmed to explain that not only had he and Michael not bonded, but the last time they saw each other, Michael wanted to kill Charlie.

The Sage continued. "One of the other children I sent out said they saw Michael in the courtyards of the

House of Lumina. That's where the Sovereign, Julian, resides." The Sage paused. "The Sovereign is your father, Charlie, and the greatest evil this world has ever seen."

Charlie stiffened. "My father?"

"Yes. I know this is a lot for you take in, but both your father and your mother, Josephine, are here in Lumina. They are alive."

Charlie covered his mouth with his hand. "They're alive?" he said from behind his fingers. His mind whirled.

"Yes," the Sage said, "And I'm afraid there's more, Charlie. The Sovereign has imprisoned your mother."

Charlie felt his eyes widen.

"And the entire world of Eydon is under a curse from his dark power. I brought you and your brother, Michael, here to help save this world and its people. But with your brother now in the hands of the Sovereign ..." The Sage shook his head. "I can only assume Michael will be of no use to us." He drew a deep breath, leaned forward, and held Charlie's gaze. "That leaves you."

A lightheaded feeling washed over Charlie. He was dizzy.

The Sage cleared his throat. "You and your brother are the last two heirs in the bloodline of the Guardians of the Keys," he said.

The room spun, and Charlie shoved back from the table.

The Sage drew out his next words. "Which means you, Charlie, are the last hope of Lumina."

"Last hope of Lumina," the parrot repeated. It shuffled down the Sage's arm and crossed the table toward Charlie. The bird stared at him, cocked its head, then said again, "Last hope of Lumina."

"Yes, Winny, I believe he heard you," the Sage said.

Charlie stood, legs unsteady.

"No," he said, shaking his head. "No, no, no. None of this make sense." He wavered on his feet. "You don't understand. I'm an orphan. I don't have parents. I don't have a twin brother. And Michael? Well, he hates me. Wants to kill me even. No." Charlie shook his head again. "You've got the wrong guy. I'm not the last hope of anything."

Charlie's breath came in great gasping gulps.

The Sage nodded, then pushed back in his chair. He cast a glance at Brynn. "Why don't you make yourself comfortable in one of the spare rooms."

Brynn nodded, and the Sage stood. The ferret leapt to the ground and scurried away.

"Charlie, you look like you could use some fresh air." The Sage held out an arm for the parrot to climb, then motioned for Charlie to follow. "Come," he said. "Let's take a walk."

CHAPTER TEN

OUTSIDE THE COTTAGE, Charlie felt his bearings return. The earth felt solid under his feet again, and his mind cleared. But in the darkened star-studded world of Lumina, Charlie still couldn't help but think that none of this was real.

"I'm pretty sure I'm dreaming," he said. "Maybe I ate a bad mango back on the island or something."

The moonlight illuminated the Sage's smirk and highlighted the iridescent feathers in his beard. "I can see how you might think so," the Sage said as he led Charlie toward a lookout point on the hillside. "But I assure you this isn't a dream. After all, you know precisely how you got here—through the portal on the island. If you didn't know how you'd arrived, well, that's when we might start questioning your reality. Isn't that right, Winny?" the Sage said to the parrot perched on his arm.

The parrot bobbed up and down.

Charlie shook his head. "I don't understand."

The Sage waved his words away. "Don't mind us," he said with a smile and a wink to the parrot. He paused when they reached the lookout.

A circular, torchlit city surrounded the towering spire Charlie had seen from the rooftop. Above it, a brilliant full moon cast the only other light.

"Wow," Charlie said. "The city looks pretty incredible from up here."

"Looks can be deceiving," the Sage said. The parrot climbed from his arm onto his shoulder. "That there is a city lost in great darkness." The Sage folded his arms over his chest.

"What do you mean?" Charlie asked.

The Sage turned to look at him. "You've been through a lot today, Charlie. Are you sure you're ready for this story and all the darkness it entails? I don't want to overwhelm you any more than you already are."

Charlie considered the Sage's question, then drew a deep breath. "Yes," he said. "Tell me about Lumina."

A warm smile emerged from under the Sage's thick mustache. "I was hoping you'd say that. Here, let's have a seat." He motioned for Charlie to join him on the ground. A blanket of stars glimmered above them.

Though the Sage's hair was gray and his face weathered, there was a youthfulness to his demeanor. He seemed agile and spry, like he was once a great warrior who'd made every effort to preserve his physical strength. When he rolled up the sleeves of his tunic, Charlie noted the sinewy muscles that lined his arms. The Sage crossed his legs beneath him, and Charlie did the same.

"Up here, Lumina appears to be a charming city with its subtle warm glow," the Sage said. "But if you'd spent any time on her streets, you might think differently."

Charlie nodded. "I met the Sovereign Guard."

"Oh, so you do know then. Yes, as you may have guessed, the Sovereign Guard is in service to your father." The Sage paused. "But I'm getting ahead of myself."

He cleared his throat. "For one hundred fifty years, Lumina was a great and noble city—"

The parrot squawked. "One hundred fifty years," it repeated. "One, two, three—"

The Sage burst into laughter. He raised a hand to his shoulder, and the parrot stepped onto the back of his fingers. With his other hand, he stroked the bird's feathers.

"Yes, yes, good boy. But we need to work on your timing." He spoke softly to the parrot. "Now, I'm about to tell Charlie a story."

Winny seemed to perk up.

"Would you like to hear a story?"

The parrot dipped his head.

"Ah, then you must be quiet"—the Sage placed a finger over his lips—"and listen." He touched his ear.

"Quiet and listen," Winny repeated.

"Very good," the Sage said to his feathered friend, then leaned in and made a soft chirping noise. The parrot nuzzled his beak into the Sage's beard.

Charlie watched their curious exchange.

"Oh!" the Sage said as if remembering Charlie was beside him. "You'll have to forgive me. These days I spend most of my time with animals. That's what happens when you're in hiding, but never mind that. Now where was I?"

Winny answered. "One hundred fifty years," he said.

"Oh, yes. Very good. Thank you." The Sage stroked his beard. "For one hundred fifty years, Lumina was a great and noble city ruled by love, peace, and harmony. It was a city of light, not a world of darkness. In fact, the light illuminated all twelve cities of Eydon. It was a wonderful place, Charlie."

The moonlight revealed a faraway look in the Sage's eyes. He pointed. "You see that spire there? These days, the only light Lumina sees is the faint flicker of torch and flame, but twenty-six years ago, that was not the case. Then, the Light of the World dwelled within that spire."

"The Light of the World?" Charlie asked. "Sounds like something I read in religion class."

"Yes," the Sage said. "But here in Lumina, the Light of the World was a giant glowing orb, placed here by the Father of Lights when he established the city. Its radiance was purer than anything you've ever seen."

The Sage cast a sidelong glance in Charlie's direction. "One thing you must remember, Charlie, is that the things you know as spiritual from the other world manifest as physical here. I suspect you learned a great deal about the spiritual reality during your brief time at Saint Francis's Boys and Girls Home?"

"I guess so," Charlie said.

"Good." The Sage nodded. "That knowledge will prove useful here." He tapped Winny on the beak. "But back to the story," he said with a grin.

"In the beginning of Eydon, there was the Light of the World. And that light was the light in all humankind." The Sage gestured to the city. "It filled that spire with its brilliance and cast its glow on the entire capital city of Lumina and into every human heart. It even kindled eleven reflecting lights in the spires of each of the other eleven cities. No one in all of Eydon was deprived of the light's brilliance and warmth."

Charlie mind swirled with wonder. "So what happened to it?" he asked.

"Your *father* happened to it," the Sage said in a low voice.

Charlie swallowed and waited for him to continue.

"In that spire, three pedestals form a triangle, and on top of each one, there used to be a key."

"A key like you'd use to open a door?" Charlie asked.

The Sage shook his head. "No, more like a precious gemstone." He held up his thumb and forefinger to show the size. "About two inches long, diamond shaped. They're beautiful, and together, these three keys form the Trinity of Limitless Power."

Charlie's mind spun with questions.

The Sage continued. "The Guardians of the Keys, which I mentioned to you, served in the House of Lumina. Their job was to guard the keys, for if even one was stolen, darkness could shroud the light, blocking it from all humanity."

The Sage stared at the city below. "Which is exactly what happened. Your parents, Julian and Josephine, were descendants in the bloodline of the guardians and began their service in their thirtieth year. But unbeknownst to anyone, Julian had already chosen the darkness."

As the Sage spoke, a thick cloud drifted across the sky and masked the moon. Winny peered up at the darkness, then ruffled his feathers like he was shaking off a chill.

"Many years before Julian's inauguration of service, a wicked being, disguised as a snake, came to him in a dream and tempted him with lies of power, wealth, and the knowledge of light and darkness. The snake promised Julian that if he stole the keys and concealed the light, he would finally understand and gain true power."

The Sage drew a deep breath and turned to look at Charlie. "And so he did."

Charlie looked away.

"On the day Julian stole the keys, darkness descended on the land like an oppressive cloud. It began at the House of Lumina, first shrouding the orb with a thick, impenetrable layer of stone. Then the darkness spread throughout the city. Eventually, it filled the entire world of Eydon."

"Is that why it's always so dark here?" Charlie asked.

"Correct," the Sage said. "But it's not just physically dark, Charlie." He shook his head. "Oh no. The true darkness is the spiritual darkness that hides the light in every human heart, like a basket placed over a candle, hiding the light away. Have you noticed the people's eyes?"

Charlie nodded.

"They're blind, Charlie. Blind to the Light of the World. Which is why we need you."

"Me?"

"Yes, Charlie. *You.*" The Sage turned to face him fully. He leaned forward and grabbed Charlie's arm. His clear blue eyes burned with intensity. "Because while the Sovereign thinks he's won, the truth is that light can only be hidden, never destroyed."

The Sage blinked, then released Charlie's arm. He chuckled. "Forgive me. Sometimes my passion for this world burns too strong." His eyes drifted toward the city once more. "I only wish to see it liberated. I've been hoping for its freedom for many years."

"You still haven't explained what this has to do with me," Charlie said.

The Sage drew a deep breath. "In this world, only a descendant in the bloodline of the guardians can uncover the light, because only someone in the bloodline can return the keys to their stands. This is why your mother brought you and your brother to me when you were babies."

Charlie looked down at his hands. The mention of his mother unraveled a tangle of emotions he'd tried to ignore for years.

"Your mother asked me to send you through the portal to another world and begged me to never bring you back."

Charlie clenched his jaw. So she'd abandoned him. Charlie had always hoped some other reason led him to become an orphan: maybe his mother had died or wasn't fit to raise him. But even still, he'd always held a thread of resentment toward her. How could any mother abandon her child?

"She didn't want me," Charlie whispered into the darkness, remembering Michael's hateful words.

"Of course she *wanted* you," the Sage said. "But she *didn't* want your father to kill you. She feared for your life. And rightfully so, it seems."

"Then why didn't she run away with us?" Charlie asked, thinking of how different his life would've been if she had.

"Because she was a guardian," the Sage said. "She'd taken a vow to protect the keys. So she stayed behind to serve with her comrades, believing that if anyone could turn Julian's heart back toward the light, it would be her."

The Sage paused. "But she failed."

The silence of the night lingered.

"Julian never killed your mother," the Sage said. "He'd loved her since he was a boy. So he imprisoned her instead. But as for the other guardians?" The Sage shook his head. "On the day your father stole the keys and cursed the land, he began a twenty-six-year massacre, hunting down and killing every last descendant in the guardians' bloodline, even children." The Sage's voice dropped. "The last of them was a young girl who'd been in hiding most of her life. She died only four days ago, in your world's time, murdered by a devout member of the Sovereign Guard, a man named Cyrus."

Charlie glanced up, setting aside the thoughts of his mother. "Four days ago?" he said. "That's when we found out about the trip to Mexico."

"Yes," the Sage nodded. "As I said, I have eyes and ears in the other world. And assistants who helped me orchestrate my plan to get you here. I promised your mother I wouldn't bring you and your brother back unless it was the only option. But after that young girl's death … Well, here we are. You are this world's only hope, Charlie."

Winny repeated his words. "Only hope."

Charlie stared at the quiet city of Lumina for several minutes before speaking. "This is all real?" he finally asked.

"Very real," the Sage said. "This is your home, Charlie."

The word *home* struck him once again.

"I have no home," Charlie whispered.

"You do," the Sage said. "Lumina is your home, and it needs you."

Charlie shook his head. "I can't do this," he said. "And even if I could, I don't know how to save a city— an entire world, even."

Empathy filled the Sage's voice. "You needn't worry about that, Charlie. You'll have plenty of guidance, and you won't be alone. All you need to do is to say yes to the quest."

"But I don't even know what the quest is."

"True." The Sage eyed him then said, "Do you want to know?"

Charlie bit his lip then said, "Maybe."

The Sage waited for him.

"I mean, I guess so," Charlie said.

The Sage dipped his head. "Very well. As I said, your father, the Sovereign, stole the three keys. To ensure their protection from the guardians he knew would oppose him, the Sovereign separated the keys and locked each one inside a cursed stronghold that no mere mortal could ever hope to penetrate. Only a guardian or a descendant in the bloodline could cross the strongholds' barriers and retrieve the keys. But as I said, there are only four living individuals left in the bloodline: the Sovereign; your mother, who is in prison; your brother, who is currently with your father"—the Sage paused—"and you. Of these four, you, Charlie, are the only one who can accept the mission. You must journey to the farthest corners of Lumina, conquer the three strongholds to retrieve the keys, and return them to their pedestals in the House of Lumina." The Sage paused. "Simple as that," he said with a chuckle.

"Simple as that," Winny said.

Charlie looked away from the Sage. "If it's so simple, then why don't you do it?"

"Because I'm no guardian, Charlie. I'm not even from this world, just here for a time. Even this cottage doesn't belong to me." He gestured in the direction of the house. "I borrowed it from an old friend who also visits the city."

Charlie could feel the Sage's stare on the side of his face.

"It *must* be you, Charlie. It has to be you."

Charlie finally looked at him. "You wouldn't be asking me to do this if you knew me."

A broad smile spread across the Sage's bearded face. "Ah, but you see, I *do* know you, Charlie. Perhaps even better than you know yourself. It sounds like it's *you* who doesn't know yourself."

"That doesn't make any sense," Charlie said.

"I know." The Sage grinned. "But it will."

The sound of crickets filled the quiet.

"I understand you're afraid, Charlie. And that this is a lot to take in. I can only imagine the thoughts racing through your mind. But I also know what you're capable of, because I see the light within you. You have what it takes, Charlie."

His words stirred Charlie's memory.

Michael's voice filled his mind.

You don't have what it takes, he heard Michael say. *To be in the Abbott family—or any family for that matter.*

In that moment on the island, when Michael had spoken those words, Charlie knew Michael was right.

Charlie didn't belong in the Abbott family, and he certainly didn't belong in any special bloodline.

Even his own mother saw him unfit to stay in her home and in this land, as if she knew he'd never be able to succeed in such a quest.

"You won't be alone," the Sage continued. "Brynn will go with you." He leaned over and grabbed Charlie's arm once again. The intensity returned to his eyes. They burned like the torches that lit the darkened city. "But you must move quickly, Charlie," the Sage said in a hurried tone. "You are this world's last chance. Everything rides on you—the destiny of this world *and* the other. You leave at dawn."

"The other?"

"Your friends on the island," the Sage said.

Charlie yanked his arm away and jumped to his feet. "I can't," he said, shaking his head. "This is all too much. You may think you know me; you may think I have what it takes, but I don't."

The Sage scrambled to his feet. "But, Charlie, I—"

"No. I'm sorry." Charlie's voice cracked. "I just can't do it."

He turned to walk back to the cottage. Under his breath he said to himself, "I *don't* have what it takes."

The Sovereign crossed the polished marble floor of his private chambers. Torchlight glinted off the gold décor and warmed the thick velvet curtains that draped the walls in midnight blue. The fabric muffled the echo of Julian's heavy footsteps. He paused beside the window and gazed out at the dimly lit streets of Lumina. The muscles in Julian's jaw twitched. He interlaced his fingers behind his back.

The door to his bed chambers opened. "My lord?" It was the Chancellor's voice. "You called for me."

Julian didn't bother to turn or acknowledge him. Instead, he waited for the sound of the Chancellor's footsteps to approach. He heard the man stop behind him.

Julian inhaled, forcing an outward calm to hide the rage that boiled beneath the surface. "You checked on the boy?" he asked.

"I did."

"And?"

"He seems quite uncomfortable in the dungeons, my lord."

"Good," Julian said coldly.

"Will that be all, my lord?" the Chancellor asked.

Julian clenched his teeth, taking a moment before responding. "I've served as the Sovereign of Lumina for twenty-six years," he said. "And I am *not* about to give up my kingdom. Especially not because of two young boys."

"Of course, my lord," the Chancellor said. "You've overcome far greater threats than these."

Julian nodded, his eyes fixed on the city. Over the years, he had faced countless threats, all influenced by one—the Sage. Julian closed his eyes and drew a sharp breath through his nostrils. "I've made my decision about the boy," he said.

"Shall I arrange for him to be sent to the gallows in the morning?" the Chancellor asked. "We could make a spectacle of it—send a message to the Sage and—"

"That won't be necessary," Julian said. He turned from the window, crossed the room, and paused before an arched wooden door. Running his fingers across its carved panels, Julian imagined the stone tunnel on the other side and the winding flight of stairs that led to the top of the spire—to the pinnacle of the House of Lumina and the shrouded orb that resided within it.

"Forgive me, my lord," the Chancellor said. "But isn't it necessary to kill the boy?"

Julian turned to look at the Chancellor. "Of course it's necessary to kill him," he said. "But not yet. He may prove to be useful."

"How so?" the Chancellor asked.

Julian crossed the room and took a seat on the end of his ornate four-poster bed. He ran a finger over one of the black hand-carved wooden posts.

"We know that my other son, Charles, is alive and came through the portal." Julian furrowed his brow in disgust. "And we also know the Sage is involved. There's no other explanation for how the boys could have returned."

The Chancellor nodded.

Julian continued. "I suspect the Sage will waste no time in sending Charles to the strongholds to retrieve the keys. For all we know, he's already on his way to the first one."

"But he's just a boy," the Chancellor said. "Surely, the journey alone would be too much for him. Even if he did manage to reach the first stronghold, I'm certain it would destroy him. After all, my lord, you created the strongholds."

Julian nodded. "Precisely. I created them, but these boys are *my sons*. They have what it takes to physically survive the strongholds, as only guardians do. I'm concerned Charles may also have his father's perseverance. This is a risk I can't take. If he enters the strongholds, only someone else in the bloodline can go in after him. Other than their mother who is hidden away, there is only one still alive in our bloodline."

"Michael," the Chancellor said.

Julian nodded. He fixed his eyes on the arched doorway. Even here he could feel the subtle throb of power from the shrouded orb two stories above his private bed chambers. Ever since he ushered in the shroud, Julian was physically bound to its power, unable to venture beyond the courtyard walls of the House of Lumina.

If he did, he would die.

He nearly had the first time he tried to leave the property.

"Yes," Julian said. "If Charles goes after the keys, then Michael is the only one who can stop him." He paused dramatically. "So rather than eliminate Michael now, I'll use him to destroy the threat of Charles, then dispose of Michael as I see fit."

A sinister smile spread across the Chancellor's face. "You are wise, my lord," he said. "And a worthy ruler." He bowed. "It shall be my honor to help you carry out your plan. Though, I must admit, I'm a bit disappointed we'll have to delay the gallows."

Julian gave the man a hard stare. "No need to

gloat, Chancellor," he said. "It's a gruesome task we undertake."

He hesitated for a long beat, considering the lengths he had already gone to for the sake of his power. And now, with this final blow, that power would be secured forever. By bringing the boys back, the Sage had unwittingly played into his hands.

Julian stood and strode for the exit. "Tomorrow we send Michael to stop Charles at the first stronghold before we eliminate them both. Then you may have your gallows."

"And if the boy refuses to go?" the Chancellor said behind him.

"He won't," Julian said without turning back. "I know his heart. After all, he is my son."

CHAPTER ELEVEN

CHARLIE SAT UP IN BED and glanced around the small cottage bedroom. After Charlie had fled their conversation on the hillside, the Sage had followed him inside and promised to take him to the portal in the morning—if that's what Charlie wanted.

Now, leaning against the headboard, Charlie wondered if it *was* morning. It was impossible to tell with the perpetual darkness outside the bedroom window. But it felt like hours had passed since he'd crawled beneath the lavender-scented sheets and drifted off to sleep. Feeling hungry, he swung his legs over the side of the bed, then wandered out of the guest room.

Down the hall, Brynn's door was open, as was the door to the Sage's room. Both bedrooms appeared empty as Charlie passed. Silence lingered in the cottage, broken only by the creak of the wooden floorboards beneath Charlie's feet. The gentle tick of a clock greeted him in the main room, accompanied by the chirp of crickets that drifted in through an open window. But there was no sign of the Sage or Brynn.

Charlie crossed the room and noticed a wooden bowl on the table, and beside it, a note.

Good morning, Charlie. (Yes, it's morning!) There's a pot of oatmeal over the fire. I will return shortly. Please make yourself at home.

Charlie's stomach roared at the thought of food. He felt even hungrier than he had the night before. He filled the bowl to the brim with steaming oatmeal, then ventured outside to the old wooden rocking chair he'd noticed on the porch. The scent of cinnamon and vanilla wafted up from the bowl. Steam warmed his face as Charlie made himself comfortable in the rocker beneath the Lumina Lilies. He peered out at the hillside where he'd talked with the Sage and scooped a large bite into his mouth. The white ferret appeared out of nowhere and jumped onto his lap, causing him to fumble the bowl. The creature placed its tiny paws on the rim, peered inside at the oatmeal, then stared at Charlie.

From the corner of his eye, Charlie saw a figure climbing the hillside. He sat up straighter.

"Hey, Charlie."

It was Brynn.

"Hey," he said, then took a bite of oatmeal. The ferret didn't take his eyes off him, waiting for Charlie to share his meal.

"You slept late," Brynn said.

Charlie glanced at the sky. "Did I?"

He saw her grin flash in the moonlight. "Yeah, it's already after ten—*in the morning*," she added with a chuckle.

Charlie scooped another spoonful of oatmeal into his mouth, then asked, "What are you doing out here?"

She sat on the porch's top step near the rocking chair.

"I'll show you," she said as she produced a small jar from the pocket of her tunic.

Tiny flashes of red light pulsed inside the glass, drawing the attention of the ferret, who jumped down from Charlie's lap for a closer inspection.

Charlie set his bowl down. "What are those?"

"Torch beetles," Brynn said, holding up the jar. "They used to be common, but they're kind of hard to find now. I can usually only find them up here in the mountains."

Charlie watched the inch-long beetles wriggle along the inside of the glass. There were four. Brynn unscrewed the lid and let one climb up her finger. The beetle's body was a deep red and glimmered with an iridescent sheen. Every few seconds, it pulsed with a warm glow. It reminded Charlie of a lightning bug.

"What are you going to do with them?" he asked.

Brynn returned the beetle to the jar with the other three and tightened the lid.

"I sell them in town," she said. "I can usually get enough money from one to buy a loaf of bread." She held up the jar. "So this is four days' worth of food. A week if I stretch it." She tucked the jar back into her pocket.

Charlie glanced down at his nearly empty bowl of oatmeal, realizing that the warm welcome Brynn received from the Sage probably wasn't her everyday experience.

"What do people do with the beetles after they buy them?" Charlie asked.

Brynn peered up at him. The torchlight glimmered in her milky-gray eyes, and Charlie remembered what the Sage had said about the people of this world.

"Usually they put the beetles in a terrarium and keep them as pets." She shrugged. "They're supposedly good luck." She stood and motioned for Charlie to follow her into the grass. "Here, I'll show you how to find them."

She handed Charlie a stick and started digging with

another. "Now, if I could just find a solarfly, I'd be able to buy enough food for a year," she said.

Charlie followed Brynn's lead and prodded the dirt with the stick. "What's a solarfly?" he asked, while shooing the ferret out of his way.

Brynn flipped her braided red hair over her shoulder. "Oh, just a myth," she said. "They're not real. Solarflies are *supposedly* glowing butterflies."

Charlie paused his digging and stared at her.

Brynn didn't notice. "But if they *were* real," she said, "I'm sure I could get a lot of money for one." She didn't look up from the dirt. "When I was little, my mom told me solarflies existed during the time of the light." Brynn shook her head. "But I don't know if I believe that. I think they're both just myths—the light and the solarflies."

Charlie's thoughts drifted to the glowing butterfly that had led him to Lumina—and the many others he'd seen throughout his life. He watched Brynn pry a small rock out of the dirt and decided not to tell her about them—not yet at least. "You mentioned your mom," he said to her, "but the Sage said you're an orphan."

Without looking up, Brynn nodded. "Yeah, my parents died when I was little. They were murdered." She finally glanced up at him. "By the Sovereign Guard. My parents believed in the Legend of the Light." Her long red braid fell over one shoulder. "My parents were a part of a rebel group that hid people who were in the bloodline of the guardians. When the Sovereign issued an edict to kill everyone in the bloodline, he also killed anyone who helped them." She paused. "I was six years old when it happened. I'm twelve now."

Charlie shook his head in disbelief. "That's terrible." Then a wave of guilt washed over him. Charlie's father had killed Brynn's parents because they were hiding members of the guardian bloodline—people like him.

He locked eyes with her, then lowered his voice. "I'm so sorry, Brynn."

She offered him a forced smile. "Thanks. I'd do anything to have them back." She looked away and said, "At least your parents are still alive."

A beat of silence lingered in the wake of her words.

"Yeah," Charlie whispered, unsure how to sort through the tangle of emotions he felt about that and his mother's abandonment—a truth he'd always known but refused to fully believe. Until now.

"You must be excited to get back home," Brynn said, changing the subject.

"Back home?" Charlie asked.

"Yeah, home." Brynn continued digging in the dirt. "Back to wherever you're from. The Sage told me you're going back. He said you weren't going to stay and save Lumina."

Despite his full belly, a pit formed in Charlie's stomach. "Look, I'm really sorry about your parents, Brynn, and your city," Charlie hesitated, "but I can't do this."

"Oh, you don't have to explain it to me," Brynn said. "I get it."

"You do?"

"Of course," she said. "Why risk your life for a legend?"

Her words stirred him. "But your parents did," Charlie said. "And the Sage said you'd be going with me if I said yes to this mission."

"I know," Brynn said matter-of-factly. "But I wasn't doing it for the legend. I was doing it for my parents."

She was silent for several minutes before she asked, "So what's it like where you're from? Do you have a lot of friends? A nice house?"

Her questions unsettled him.

"Actually, my life isn't that great." An image of Sarah's face filled Charlie's mind. "I don't have any friends." His mind drifted to the island. "Or a home."

For the first time it occurred to Charlie that he had nothing to go back to. The only benefit he could see was that he'd be returning to a world without Michael.

That is, if Michael stayed here in Lumina.

The Sage said Michael was with his father—*their father*—an idea Charlie couldn't get used to.

He sighed. "Yeah, there's nothing special waiting for me back in the other world. I'm just an orphan like you."

Brynn threw the stick to the side and shoved a finger into the hole she'd dug. A second later, she dragged out a torch beetle. The ferret nosed her hand excitedly. Brynn smiled, pulled out the jar, and tucked the beetle inside with the others. She crossed her legs and closed the lid, then leaned back on one hand.

A crease formed on her brow, and a look of concern washed over her face. "I don't think you're an orphan like me at all, Charlie," Brynn said. She rubbed the ferret's back with her other hand. "I may not have parents or a warm bed every night, but I have friends. Lots of them, in fact. And I have a home." She gestured around at the hillside. "Lumina is my home." She paused. "It may be dark here, Charlie, but your world sounds much darker."

Charlie started to respond then stopped, seeing the shadowy figure of the Sage approach from over the hillside. The man carried a tall walking stick in his right hand and a small torch in his left. Winny perched on his shoulder.

"Good morning, Charlie," the Sage said as he neared them. He stopped beside them. "Ah, I see Brynn is teaching you how to dig for torch beetles—a skill that won't transfer over to your world, I'm afraid." He chuckled.

"I have five so far," Brynn said with a broad smile.

"Wonderful." The Sage patted her on the head. "That should fetch you five loaves. I think I have some extra cheese in the cottage. Why don't you take it with you when you leave?"

Brynn nodded.

"Where are you going?" Charlie asked her.

"Back into town." She stood and brushed the palms of her hands against her pants. "My work here is done."

"As is mine," the Sage said. "Charlie, are you ready to go? We can leave for the portal after you say your good-byes to Brynn."

Charlie hesitated, thinking of Brynn's words.

Was his world truly so much darker than this one?

"What will happen to Michael if I leave?" Charlie asked.

The Sage leaned on his walking stick. "I don't know. What happens to Michael here in Lumina is up to Michael. He's with your father now. I have no influence over him."

The Sage paused and searched Charlie with his eyes. "But, Charlie, what happens to *you* here in Lumina is also up to you. I won't force you into anything. Whatever you decide, it must be *your* choice. But you must also know something." He paused. "Your choice affects the children on the island as well."

Charlie stiffened. "What do you mean?"

"The island and Lumina are connected. The darkness from this world has, and will continue to, seep through the portal. If you accept the mission here, you're also choosing to save the island. If you refuse this mission, you doom the island as well."

The Sage waited for a response. When Charlie gave him none, he said, "I know you've always felt alone, Charlie, and like you don't belong. You were separated from your family, sent to live in a world that wasn't your own. But you've never been alone. I have remembered you. Your mother, I'm certain, has never forgotten you."

Charlie looked away.

"And this world, though lost in great darkness, still has a glimmer of remembrance for the light that dwells within you. And that light is just the thing we need to save this world, the place where you *do* belong. But the choice is yours."

Still seated on the ground, Charlie glanced up at Brynn. She clutched the jar of torch beetles against her chest, their soft red flicker visible between the gaps in her fingers.

Brynn had said the solarflies were a myth, a story like the legend of the Light of the World. But Charlie had seen them—followed one, in fact, through a portal and into this mysterious, dreamlike world.

What if the solarflies weren't just a legend?

And what if Brynn's parents didn't die for a myth but for something more?

Something real.

Brynn's parents had risked their lives to save Charlie's bloodline.

Could Charlie risk his life to save Brynn's home?

His home?

A thought occurred to him. Perhaps the reason Charlie had never felt he belonged anywhere was because he was made for a different world and a greater mission.

Charlie looked to the Sage. "How difficult will the strongholds be?"

"They will challenge you to your very core."

That didn't sound good. Not at all.

"I still don't think I can do this," he said. "And I'll probably fail."

A smile tugged at the Sage's bearded lips. "Are you always so confident in your own failures? I believe in you, Charlie." The Sage cast a glance at Brynn. "And I know Brynn does too. I doubt she would've agreed to go with you otherwise."

Brynn took a step toward Charlie and extended a hand to him. She pulled him to his feet.

"I do believe in you, Charlie," Brynn said. "Because that's what friends do." She offered him a warm smile.

Her words pierced his heart like an arrow, reminding him of Sarah.

There was no home for Charlie apart from Lumina, and no friends who were waiting for him in the other world.

But here was one.

And she believed in him.

And in that moment, Charlie believed in her.

He drew a deep breath, closed his eyes, and exhaled. When he opened his eyes, Brynn and the Sage met him with encouraging smiles.

"All right," Charlie said. "Tell me what I need to do."

CHAPTER TWELVE

WITH SHACKLED HANDS, Michael followed the guard Cyrus down the marble aisle toward the black throne where he'd met the Sovereign—his father—the day before. Today, the seat was empty.

Though he'd only met his father yesterday, Michael already hated him. For his entire life, Michael had wondered about his parents, longing to someday find them. Now that day had come, and it was worse than anything he could've imagined.

Michael's father had rejected him, thrown him into a cold, damp dungeon. He'd hardly slept, terrified of the fate that awaited him. Now confusion mingled with his fear and magnified the rage he felt at discovering that Charlie was his twin brother.

Michael sneered. Since the day he'd met Charlie, Michael knew there was something off about that boy. Knowing that he and Charlie shared the same blood only made his hatred worse.

The door in the wall behind the throne opened, and the Chancellor stepped out, carrying a stack of clothes. He waited as Michael and Cyrus made their approach.

"The Sovereign requests your presence at breakfast this morning," the Chancellor said.

Michael's stomach growled. He hadn't eaten since … He wasn't sure when. But he knew, whenever it was, he hadn't eaten more than a couple of mangos and a banana.

"Remove his shackles," the Chancellor said to Cyrus.

The Sovereign Guard obeyed.

The Chancellor handed Michael a pair of black pants with a matching tunic. Stacked on top was a midnight-blue velvet robe. "You may wear this. There's a changing room over there." The Chancellor pointed to a door in the far-right wall. "We'll wait here for your return."

Michael took the clothes, grateful for something clean to wear and returned a few minutes later.

The Chancellor straightened his shoulders. "You look regal, my lord," he said. "Here, for your feet." He handed Michael a new pair of boots.

Michael knelt to remove his sneakers and laced up the new black leather shoes. When he stood, he felt different. Perhaps regal, as the Chancellor had suggested, but more like a child playing dress-up. It was hard for Michael to understand why, after a cold night in the dungeon, he was now being addressed as "my lord" and wearing clothes fit for a king.

"Right this way," the Chancellor said and led Michael through the mysterious door in the back wall.

They entered what looked to be the Sovereign's private chambers. A massive bed sat at one end of the room, made from wood as black as the Sovereign's throne—as black as the tree Michael had seen on the island. Velvet fabrics the same color as the robe Michael now wore draped the walls. Ornaments of gold decorated every surface, but in the center of the back wall was a plain wooden door. It was simple, yet Michael found himself drawn to it.

"Would you care to join me?" The Sovereign's voice interrupted Michael's thoughts.

He stood beside a large picture window that overlooked the dark city. A table, covered in food, sat in front of the window, and the Sovereign motioned for Michael to join him and take a seat.

Michael didn't move.

"You would be wise to obey the Sovereign," the Chancellor said.

Michael saw Cyrus touch the hilt of the dagger at his waist. "Yes, it would be wise," the guard said.

Clenching his jaw, Michael crossed the room,

pulled out a chair from the table, and sat.

"Leave us," the Sovereign said to the Chancellor and Cyrus.

The two men exited.

Michael watched the Sovereign take a seat across from him, noting once again the facial features they shared. But this time he also noticed the subtle similarities to Charlie's appearance: the Sovereign's thin lips and defined nose.

The scent of the meal drew Michael's attention to the table, piled with breads and pastries, cured meats and sausages, and a bowl of hard-boiled eggs. A towering platter of fruit sat in the center. Thankfully, there were no mangos or bananas.

"You'll have to forgive me, my son," the Sovereign said. "You must understand that a man in my position can't be too careful. I have a kingdom to protect. It was necessary to hold you in the dungeons for the night. I had to be certain of your loyalties."

"And you're certain of them now?" Michael asked with a scoff. He tried not to look at the food.

"Not yet," the Sovereign said. "But I hope to be certain after our meal together." He gestured to the food. "Please eat."

Michael eyed the bread. His mouth watered, but he touched nothing.

The Sovereign shrugged, then selected a large roll

and began cutting it in half. "I see the clothes fit." He spread a thick layer of butter over the warm bread. "They suit you. You look like the son of a royal." He selected a thick slice of cured ham and folded it neatly onto the roll, smushed the two halves together, then took a large bite. Grease dripped down his chin and disappeared into his blond beard. He continued to speak while chewing. "Yesterday, you looked more like a spy in your tattered clothes."

"A spy?" Michael asked.

The sovereign wiped the grease from his chin with his hand. "Yes. We have a large population of orphans here in our city. Those children are not to be trusted. The Sage uses them to do his bidding. Years ago, some of them even helped to hide my enemies right here within my city bounds."

The Sovereign paused.

"But that was before I killed all my enemies," he said with a menacing grin. "Now, only one enemy remains."

His cold, cloudy stare pierced Michael. "Or are there two?"

"I don't know what you're talking about," Michael said.

The Sovereign flashed him a greasy smile. "Well, we don't know which side you're on yet." The Sovereign glanced out the window at the torchlit city.

"The Sage has been out to overthrow my reign since

the day it began. He's the one who brought you and your brother through the portal. Yesterday evening, I received word from my Sovereign Guard that they spotted a young boy with brown skin and golden eyes running through the streets of Lumina with one of those pesky street urchins. They got away. So I have reason to believe your brother is now with the Sage, having his mind filled with lies."

"Lies about what?" Michael asked.

"About me, of course," the Sovereign said. "That I'm an unfit ruler who needs to be overthrown. And that your brother, Charles, is capable of such a task."

"Of course he's not capable of that," Michael said. "Trust me, I know."

The Sovereign leaned forward and placed an elbow on the table. He cupped his chin in his hand. "Tell me about your brother."

"He's a loser," Michael spat. "He's not even fit to be called my brother."

"So he's your enemy then?" the Sovereign asked. There was a twitch of a smile in the corner of his lips.

Michael leaned toward the Sovereign. "He's everything I hate."

The Sovereign leaned back in his chair and stroked his beard. "Interesting. We have a common enemy, then."

Michael narrowed his gaze and considered the

Sovereign's words. "You said Charlie is with the Sage, having his mind filled with lies."

The Sovereign nodded.

Michael hesitated then asked, "So what's the truth?"

A full smile spread across the Sovereign's face. "I'm so glad you asked." He pushed back in his chair, then stood. "Come, my son. Let me show you something."

The Sovereign grabbed a bread roll and handed it to Michael as he led him to the plain wooden door.

Michael ripped off a bite with his teeth and chewed hungrily. He stopped when they reached the door.

A subtle thrum pulsed in the air.

He took a step closer.

A buzz of electricity prickled his skin.

Michael dropped the roll and placed both hands on the flat surface of the door. "What is that?" he asked in a hushed voice. The vibration pulsed in his body and tingled in his fingertips.

"You feel it?" the Sovereign asked.

Michael pressed his cheek to the door. Now he could hear the thrum as well.

"Do you want to know what it is?" the Sovereign asked.

Michael leaned his whole body against the door. It was warm. "Yes," he said, feeling inexplicably drawn to the strange sensation.

"Then come with me."

The Sovereign pulled Michael out of the way, swung open the door, then led him into a stone tunnel blacker than a moonless night. It took a moment for Michael's eyes to adjust, but eventually he could see the outline of a spiral staircase in the hall.

"Years ago, there was no human ruler in this land," the Sovereign said.

He struck a match against the stone wall, then kindled a torch Michael hadn't realized was there. The Sovereign left it in its stand, then continued forward.

"Instead, a guiding force—a light—ruled Eydon and all her cities. Everyone had access to this power, but no one controlled it. Only a select group of individuals, of which I was one, ensured the power remained available to all. I was deceived then, believing every human fit to access such a force."

Michael saw the Sovereign shake his head in the dim light.

"But then I became enlightened," he said, beginning to mount the spiral staircase.

"What do you mean?" Michael asked, feeling the pulse of the vibration grow stronger with every step he climbed.

"A powerful being came to me in a dream," the Sovereign said, "warning me of the dangers of an uncontrolled force such as the one that resided here in the House of Lumina. The light was too powerful an energy. If it fell into the wrong hands, well, the results to Lumina could be devastating. This being told me I had been chosen to rule the light and the entire realm of Eydon, and with that responsibility would come great authority and power." The Sovereign cast a glance over his shoulder. "And an inheritance I could pass on to my sons."

The Sovereign arrived at the top of the staircase and stopped at a door on the landing.

The thrum of whatever lay on the other side pulsed audibly in Michael's ears. He followed the Sovereign through the doorway and into a ten-by-ten-foot open tower. Each of its four stone walls featured an arched opening that looked out at a black, starry sky. Fresh air filtered in through the windows, and Michael realized they were standing in the spire of the House of Lumina.

He took a step and fixed his eyes on the source of the thrum. A large stone orb hovered in the center of the chamber, and three pedestals formed a triangle around it. Each one had a small diamond-shaped imprint on the top. Michael watched the Sovereign approach the sphere.

"Would you like to touch it?" The Sovereign asked.

Michael felt his head nod.

His feet carried him to the orb, and Michael

watched his hand hesitate to reach out, as if it were not his own. The Sovereign wrapped his fingers around Michael's wrist, then pressed his palm against the surface.

Electricity coursed up Michael's arm. It flooded his body, then settled in his brain, alighting every neuron with wonder. A warm energy flooded his muscles and set his entire body aflame with power.

He couldn't bring himself to pull his hand away, so the Sovereign did.

"Well?" the Sovereign asked with a grin.

"That was incredible," Michael said.

"Now you see what a powerful force it is?"

Michael nodded.

"And why it must be guarded so it doesn't fall into the wrong hands?"

"Of course."

"A power such as this should only be wielded by those worthy of it." The Sovereign paused, then motioned for Michael to follow him to the window. The firelit city of Lumina surrounded them. The Sovereign placed a fatherly hand on Michael's shoulder. Though Michael was still angry he'd spent the night in the dungeons, he couldn't help but feel a sense of kinship to this man.

"Again, Michael, I'm sorry I had to treat you as I did yesterday, but I had to ensure you're not an enemy.

I can't let this power pass on to someone who's not aligned with me. It was always my desire to share my reign with my sons, but your mother opposed me. She wanted you and your brother to overthrow my kingdom and return this force to all the people a of Eydon."

Michael shook his head. "It's too powerful for them."

"Right. But not for us." The Sovereign nodded to the window. "Look at that city. This could all be yours, Michael, if you help me."

"Help you what?"

The Sovereign turned and pointed to the three pedestals. "Three keys can unlock the stone shroud that confines the power. They cannot be destroyed so I hid them in three guarded fortresses—strongholds. I'm certain the Sage will send your brother to seize them. If he succeeds, he could unlock the shroud and redistribute this power to the entire land once again."

"You don't know Charlie," Michael said. "He'll never succeed."

"I'm afraid your assurances aren't enough. Both you and your brother are of the bloodline of the Guardians of the Keys. He's the last threat that can oppose us. If he's persistent, he could succeed. I need you to stop him. I can't leave the House of Lumina. My place is here. I am bound to this power; my life depends on it."

The Sovereign caressed the stone-shrouded orb,

then closed his eyes. When he opened them, he said, "This is your inheritance, Michael—if you want it. But if you do claim it, you must guard it from your brother. We must assume that he's under the influence of the Sage now. If he succeeds, he'll redistribute the light to everyone and give away your inheritance."

"I won't allow that to happen," Michael said. "What do you need me to do?"

The Sovereign smiled. "Come with me."

He led Michael out of the spire, down the spiral staircase, and into his private chambers. He crossed the room to a large wooden cabinet and swung open its doors. Knives, swords, and arrows lined the shelves. A bow hung on the inside of one of the doors. Keys dangling on small hooks covered the other door. The Sovereign removed the bow and gathered the arrows. He pulled a quiver off the top shelf, placed the arrows in it, and handed it to Michael.

"The keys your brother will seek must be retrieved in order from the strongholds."

The Sovereign opened a drawer inside the cabinet, pulled out a map, then unrolled it. He pointed. "Here's the first one. It will take you two days to reach on my fastest horse." He tapped his finger against two other locations. "Here are the others, but you shouldn't need to venture there. You'll stop your brother at the first stronghold."

Michael nodded.

"I'll send one of my best men with you: Cyrus, whom you've met. But he can't enter the stronghold. Only a guardian or one of their descendants can survive the curses I've placed outside the strongholds. They will kill anyone of a lesser caliber."

Michael felt proud but unnerved at the same time.

"This bow is unique," the Sovereign said, handing it to Michael. "So long as you have your target in sight, its mark is true. Have you ever used a bow before?"

Michael nocked an arrow and drew back on the bowstring.

The Sovereign chuckled. "I'll take that as a yes."

Michael lowered the bow.

"Now," the Sovereign said, "could you kill him?"

Michael hesitated. He was aware that the hatred he'd felt for Charlie before was even greater now, in this dark fortress. In a strange way, it felt as if he was being influenced by something beyond him. But he pushed the thought away.

"Yes," he said.

"Good. Then you must leave right away. For all we know, Charles has a head start. It won't matter, though. I can see that *you* take after your father. Charles will be no match for you."

The Sovereign placed his hand on Michael's shoulder once again and this time looked him directly in the eyes. Michael still felt unsettled by their cloudy appearance, but he pushed the thought aside.

This was his father.

"One last thing," the Sovereign said. "You must understand that the strongholds greatly enhance the darkness of any who enter. Remember your true mission: kill your brother and protect your inheritance. Charles will have to overcome his darkness to succeed, but you can leverage yours to destroy him."

Michael gave a slight nod, a bit unnerved by what he might encounter in such a stronghold. "That's all I've ever wanted," he said.

Outside the hillside cottage, Charlie helped Brynn load a pack onto their horse. He adjusted the small leather pouch he wore around his waist, then brushed his hands against the khaki-colored pants the Sage had provided. He wore a matching tunic and leather boots as well. Even Brynn wore a new set of clothes, all gifted to them by the Sage for their journey.

Charlie patted the horse, then opened the leather pouch and checked, for the third time, that he had the Sage's map. A waxy coating protected it, but that would do no good if he lost the map before they even set off.

A wave of nerves washed over him.

"You look scared," Brynn said.

"Aren't you?" Charlie asked.

Brynn shrugged. "A little. But I'm excited too."

"That's because you don't have to go into the strongholds," Charlie said.

"Yeah, I guess I've got the easy part: keep you company and make sure you don't get lost." She glanced down at the map. "So where do we go first?"

Charlie pointed to the first marker. "Stronghold One: Envy."

"Envy?"

"Yeah, the Sage said each fortress has a name that relates to its curse and the challenges I'll have to overcome."

"Weird," Brynn said. "What are the other two called?"

"Judgment and Anger." Charlie folded the map and returned it to the pouch at his waist.

"Well, at least there's not a stronghold of wasps. I hate wasps!"

"Or snakes!" Charlie laughed.

The Sage approached from the other side of the cottage. "You two sound like you're ready for an adventure."

Winny perched on his shoulder. "Ready for an adventure," he repeated.

"I guess we're as ready as we'll ever be," Charlie said, staring off into the distance.

"Oh, I know you're ready," the Sage said. Charlie could see an animal following him—a knee-high batlike creature of some kind. "Everything you need for success is already inside you, my boy." There was a smile in the Sage's voice. "And you'll have excellent company."

"I agree." Brynn took a playful bow. When she stood, her eyes widened. "What is *that*?"

The light of the full moon illuminated the fluffy white creature who stepped up beside the Sage. It was about two feet tall, covered in dense fur and had large eyes. The creature shook itself like a dog shaking off water, then stretched out a pair of batlike wings.

"I'm a Roush," the creature said.

Brynn rushed toward it. "Oh my goodness, it's adorable!" She reached out to pet it.

The Roush swatted her hand away with its wing. "*It* has a name," the Roush said. "And *it* is not adorable."

Brynn backed away. "*It* also has an attitude."

The Sage chuckled. "Charlie, Brynn, this is Talli. As he already said, he's a Roush. And I believe *charming* is the term he prefers."

Talli nodded, then fixed his enormous green eyes on Charlie. "Yes, I am Talli, named after the great mystic

Talya—a legend in my world." Talli stretched out his wings and bowed. "At your service, young Charlie."

"You're going with us?" Charlie asked.

"Of course," Talli said. "Every hero needs a companion on their journey."

"But that's why I'm here," Brynn said.

A smile spread across Talli's fluffy batlike face. "Some heroes are so great they need more than one sidekick."

Charlie furrowed his brow.

"A wise observation," the Sage said with a smile to Charlie.

Talli glanced up at the Sage and nodded.

"Talli will be a unique addition to your team, Charlie," the Sage said. "Though Brynn can't enter the strongholds with you, Talli can."

"How?" Charlie asked.

"Because I'm not human," Talli said. "But you must know that I'm no guardian like you. I don't have the power to defeat a cursed stronghold. But I can offer my presence and guidance. And this." Talli leapt into the air, spun, and extended a short, birdlike foot. He lost his balance as he landed and tumbled to the ground.

Brynn stifled a laugh. "What was that?"

Talli brushed himself off with his wings. "Karate, of course. I've been studying under the great Gabil for a year now. Though, I must say it's quite difficult to execute a proper spinning back kick in the dark."

"I'd say," Brynn said. "Well, it's a good thing one of Charlie's sidekicks is used to the dark."

"And the moon is at its brightest this time of year," the Sage said. "You should hardly even need a torch."

"It's strange to be in a dark world in which all have forgotten that they're the Light of the World," Talli said. "But I'm sure I'll be myself in no time at all."

Charlie started to ask Talli what he meant, but the Sage continued. "Now, Charlie, a few reminders before you leave on your adventure." He handed Charlie a leather shoulder bag and a canteen. "First, stay hydrated and eat when you're hungry. There's an assortment of snacks in this bag for all three of you."

Charlie slung the bag over his shoulder and handed the canteen to Brynn.

"Second, remember that you must overcome the strongholds in order. What you learn in one will help you in the next."

Charlie drew a deep breath and nodded.

"Third, the strongholds will enhance the darkness within you. It's your own darkness that you will need to overcome."

Charlie wasn't entirely sure what that might look like. What darkness?

"And lastly," the Sage said, "know that you're never alone, Charlie, even in your darkest moments when you think you are. The light will always be with you because it is in you. That light will be your greatest guide."

"I don't think I understand."

"You will, Charlie. You will." The Sage clapped his hands together. "All right, now off you go," he said. "The first stronghold should take you a day and half to reach. You must hurry if you're to get there before Michael."

Charlie froze. "Michael?"

"Why, yes. I assume the Sovereign will use him to try to stop you."

"You didn't say anything about that," Charlie said, fear tinting his voice.

The Sage took a step closer. "This mission is not without danger, Charlie. You are putting your life at stake. But the consequences of not going would be far greater. The futures of this world and the other hang in the balance. And you are the key." He fixed Charlie with a stare. "Now, off you go. There's no time to waste."

Brynn draped the canteen strap over her shoulder. "C'mon," she said. She mounted the horse, then reached a hand down to help Charlie into the saddle behind her.

"Save room for me," Talli said. He jumped into the air, flapped his wings twice to clear the height of the horse, then perched atop its head. "Ah yes, it's a great view from up here."

The Sage stepped beside the horse and took Charlie's hand in his. He removed a blue feather from his beard and placed it in Charlie's palm. "I'd wish you luck, Charlie, but you don't need it." He leaned in closer, then said so only Charlie could hear, "I know you have what it takes." He flashed Charlie a broad grin, then patted the horse's rump. It took off at a trot.

Charlie cast a glance over his shoulder and watched the Sage shrink against the darkened hillside. Moonlight glimmered off his silvery hair as he vanished from sight.

Seeing him go, Charlie was quite sure that his life was about to be forever changed.

He only hoped that change didn't end in his death.

CHAPTER THIRTEEN

SARAH TOOK A SWIG from her water bottle. She'd grabbed it before leaving the beach with the rest of the group in their search for Charlie and Michael. The bottle was nearly empty now, even after refilling it in the freshwater spring they'd passed. Sweat ran down her temples, and a gritty, salty residue clung to her forehead, neck, and chest. Her legs ached with fatigue.

Three hours. Kurtis had said they'd been searching for three whole hours, and other than the bloodied sleeve from Michael's green Hawaiian print shirt, there was no trace of Charlie or Michael. And they'd covered the entire island.

After finding the bloody fabric, Sarah had suggested they split up into pairs to cover more ground. Of course Tyler had opposed her at first, then finally agreed. Becca suggested they meet back at the beach when they'd finished searching their assigned areas, and Sarah and Maxine were done.

Sarah turned to Maxine and offered her the last sip of water. The younger girl had a surprising level of endurance. But still, Sarah knew she was exhausted. They both were.

The tropical vegetation thinned in front of them, and the sound of crashing waves reached Sarah's ears.

"The beach is just ahead," she said to Maxine.

The girl handed her the empty water bottle.

"C'mon," Sarah said, feeling the ground shift from solid earth to a sand-soil mixture.

Sarah bit the inside of her lip, hating that she was returning from the search without Charlie. And terrified about what might have happened to him.

"I don't get it," she said aloud. "It's like they disappeared or something."

"I'm worried about them," Maxine said.

Sarah glanced over at her. "Me too."

"This island is kind of creepy," Maxine said, this time in a lower tone.

Sarah didn't respond. She'd been thinking the same thing.

Several silent seconds passed before Maxine said, "Sarah?"

"Yeah?"

The girl looked up at her. "Do you think Charlie really killed Michael?"

Sarah stopped and turned to face her directly. "Absolutely not. I *know* Charlie didn't kill Michael. I'm certain of it."

Maxine pressed her lips together, then asked, "But what happened to them?"

Sarah turned back in the direction of the beach. She could smell the salt in the air. "I don't know, Maxine." She forced a smile in the girl's direction. "But maybe someone else found them. Let's hurry back and find out."

They jogged the rest of the distance to the beach. Sarah's eyes scanned the shoreline as soon as she broke through the trees. The rest of the group was already there.

But Charlie and Michael were not.

An odd buzz surrounded the group. They huddled together in a small circle, voices low. When one of them spotted Sarah and Maxine, they all stopped and stared at the girls.

Becca looked furious, Joey terrified, and Raegan confused.

Tyler's face was unreadable, but his eyes never left Sarah's.

"Oh no," Sarah said under her breath.

"What?" Maxine asked, her voice filled with concern.

Sarah's stomach flipped. "I think they must have

found something." Sweat coated her palms. The walk from the tree line to the group stretched before her, each step more difficult to take. The sand pulled at her tennis shoes and slowed her pace, delaying the inevitable.

The other kids were silent when Sarah and Maxine finally reached them.

Sarah drew a deep breath then asked, "Did you find them?"

The muscles in Tyler's jaw twitched. "No."

Sarah's shoulders fell. "What? Nothing? Not even"— she paused—"not even another clue?"

"If by clue you mean incriminating evidence against Charlie, then no. We found no other signs of them." Tyler shoved his hands into his pockets.

Sarah knew Tyler was worried about his best friend. And so was she.

"So what is it then?" Sarah asked, looking from Tyler to Becca. "Something happened."

"Didn't you notice?" Becca spat.

Sarah shook her head.

"Our stuff is gone!"

Sarah furrowed her brow. Then it clicked. Her eyes widened. She turned and scanned the beach.

Their tarps, the food they'd collected, everything they'd pulled from the plane, it was all gone.

Panic squeezed Sarah's chest. "What happened to it?"

"Isn't it obvious?" Becca glared at Sarah. "Someone came to rescue us, and we weren't here!" Her voice was shrill.

"That doesn't make sense," Sarah said. "They'd come looking for us then." She pointed to the spot where their camp used to be. "And why would they take our stuff?"

"Exactly," Kurtis said. "The more logical explanation is that there's someone else on the island. Or a tide washed everything away."

"But you said there isn't anyone else on the island," Joey said.

"Unless they live underground." Milo's eyes widened as he spoke. "Or maybe they're invisible."

Raegan shot him a disgusted look. "Milo, can you just not be yourself right now?"

He shrugged. "Anything's possible on a magical island."

"It's not a magical island," Kurtis said. "There's always a logical explanation."

"Well, if it's not magical, then where'd the plane go?"

Everyone paused.

No one spoke as they followed Milo's gaze and his pointing finger.

Sarah hadn't noticed it, and, apparently, neither had the rest of the group, too consumed with their tarps and food.

Fifty meters out from the shore, where the white tail of the plane once jutted from the murky depths, there was nothing.

"Where is it?" Maxine asked.

Sarah scanned the waves. "I … I don't know."

"The sandbar could have shifted," Kurtis said. "Or the waves could have pulled it out to sea. Again, there's a logical explanation. For everything," he added.

"What's the logical explanation for Michael and Charlie then?" Milo asked. "It's like they disappeared or something."

"We already have a logical explanation for that." Tyler spoke up this time. "Isn't that right, Sarah?" He pierced her with his stare.

She felt her defenses rising. "What are you talking about?"

He stepped toward her. "I'm talking about the fact that Charlie killed Michael. And you know where Charlie's hiding."

"That's ridiculous," Sarah said.

"Is it?" Tyler jeered. "Or is it the most logical explanation?"

"Tyler," Sarah said through gritted teeth, "this is

a major accusation you're making. Against Charlie *and* me."

Tyler stepped closer and lowered his face toward hers. "Is it an accusation? Or is it the truth?"

Sarah shoved his chest. "Get out of my face, Tyler, or—"

"Or what?" Tyler glared. "Or you'll hide my body with Michael's?"

Rage flashed through Sarah's body. She shoved him with both hands.

"Sarah, don't!" Maxine was beside her, a hand on her arm.

Taking a step back, Sarah caught herself, but anger clouded her mind.

"Guys!" Becca shouted. "Fighting won't fix anything."

Tyler composed himself, but his eyes continued to pierce Sarah with a hateful stare.

Sarah looked away. "So what do we do now?" she asked, trying to shift her focus.

"Tyler," Raegan said. "Can you swim out and see if the plane is still there? Maybe it moved like Kurtis suggested."

Tyler hesitated before he said, "I guess. Sure."

"I don't think you should go out there," Becca said. "I don't think anyone should go into that water." There was an odd quality to Becca's tone that Sarah hadn't heard since the day they'd crashed. Becca was afraid, perhaps more than she'd ever been.

That's when Maxine voiced the concern that Sarah suspected lingered in the back of everyone's mind.

"If the plane's gone," Maxine began, "does that mean the transponder's gone too?"

Everyone looked to Becca. Her lips pulled into a tight line.

Kurtis answered for her. "Yes."

The group fell silent.

"So that means?"

"It means no one is coming for us," Tyler said.

"So we're stranded on an island with no supplies, no form of communication, and no transponder?" Raegan clarified.

"And Charlie and Michael are missing," Joey added.

Sarah avoided Tyler's stare. An overwhelming feeling of dread replaced the anger she had felt moments before.

The group turned and stared out at the vast ocean. Murky waters stretched as far as they could see in every direction. There wasn't even a hint of land beyond their shore.

Sarah wrapped her arms around herself and, despite the heat, shivered.

How in the world would they ever make it off this island?

The Journey Continues

BOOK TWO
THE GREAT DIVIDE

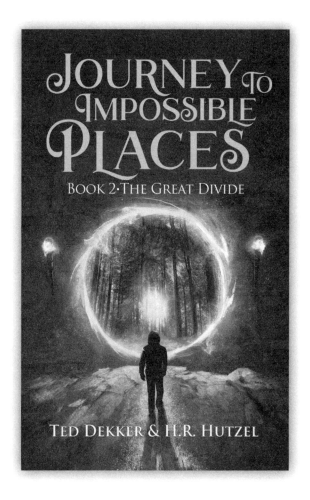

MORE ADVENTURES AWAIT

Discover the entire
Dekker young reader universe.

WWW.TEDDEKKER.COM